W9-AFJ-340

STEALING THE PLUG'S HEART

BARBIE SCOTT

Stealing the Plug's Heart

Copyright © 2019 by Barbie Scott

Published by Shan Presents
www.shanpresents.com

All rights reserved. No part of this book may be used or reproduced in any form or by any means electronic or mechanical, including photocopying, recording, or by information storage and retrieval system, without the written permission from the publisher and writer, except brief quotes used in reviews.

This is a work of fiction. Any references or similarities to actual events, real people, living or dead, or to the real locals intended to give the novel a sense of reality. Any similarity in other names, characters, places, and incidents are entirely coincidental.

SUBSCRIBE

Text Shan to 22828 to stay up to date with new releases, sneak peeks, contest, and more....

SUBMISSIONS

To submit your manuscript to Shan Presents, please send the first three chapters and synopsis to submissions@shanpresents.com

MAKAVELI

Screamin' like you dyin' every time I'm fuckin' you
Ya never had a father or a family, but I'll be there
No need to fear so much insanity, and through the years
I know ya gave me your heart, plus, When I'm dirt broke and fucked
up, ya still love me - Makaveli

PROLOGUE

CHASTITY

One would think that the weeps of a young and innocent girl would make a person have empathy. But that wasn't the case. The man that physically abused my body showed not one ounce of remorse. Instead, he pulled his camera from around his neck and, like always, he began snapping photos of my body that hadn't even developed. As tears poured from my eyes, I tried hard to cock my legs open upon his demand. The inside of my thighs were sore and my anal stung from the hour long penetration.

The sound of flicker from his camera made me cry more, but I was happy this was now coming to an end. After the last photo, he came to my bedside and whispered into my ear.

"I'll see you soon." making my insides cringe.

Everything about him was creepy and especially the scary mask he wore. I watched as he exited my bedroom and vanished into my dark home. I laid lifeless in my bed covered in my own blood as semen from him ejaculating all over my body ran onto my dirty sheets.

Pow!

. . .

THE SOUND of a loud explosion made my eyes shoot open and I became alert. I don't know where the sound had come from but I was hoping it came from my father. My father was always at work and he wasn't due until 2am but maybe tonight after 3 years, God had answered my prayers. I wanted so bad to climb out the bed but my body was numb from pain.

"Help me!" I screamed in hopes someone would hear me but my voice was muffled due to all the crying. Suddenly, the sound of someone running could be heard in my hallway then my door burst open crashing into my toy chest behind the door.

"Daddy." I began to weep harder as he ran to my bedside.

"It's okay baby, I shot that bastard." my father wrapped me in his arms and held me for a split second. Pulling me from his embrace, he looked over my body and his eyes held so much sorrow. "Chastity, you go get cleaned up. I'm gonna go get rid of his body okay."

"We have to call the police." I began to hysterically cry. I was so overwhelmed that my body continued to shake profoundly.

"No baby we can't call the police. They will take Daddy to jail. You don't want me to go to jail forever right?" I shook my head no sadly.

My hands began to shake and my legs trembled at just the thought of my father going to jail. Because my mother had been murdered he was all I had in this world. Not only was he the best father in the world but today he had become my hero. "Remember baby you are never to tell anyone about this okay?"

"Okay." I replied as my heart cringed.

"Now you go clean up." my father lifted from the bed and left the room.

Just knowing my father had killed the intruder made me feel more secure, however, I was petrified to leave my bedroom. After the torture I've been through for the past 3 years I needed my father by my side at all times. This was something I would never recover from and I would be traumatized my entire life.

∾

Legend

.   .   .

POP! Pop! Pop! Pop! Pop! Pop! Pop! Pop! Pop! Pop! Pop! Pop!
Pop! Pop! Pop! Pop! Pop! Pop! Pop! Pop! Pop! Pop! Pop! Pop!
Pop! Pop! Pop! Pop!

AS I EMPTIED ALL *my bullets towards my prey the sound of screaming could be heard from the nearby pedestrians. As I watched him fall, the sound of a screaming woman caught my attention. She fell to the ground screaming "my baby!" and it stopped me in my tracks. Normally, I'd flee the scene but it's like my body stood froze. His small feet peeked from underneath his weeping mother and no matter how much Kill screamed my name I was in a daze. I jogged over to the child that laid lifeless and my insides cringed just hearing the sounds of his mother's cries. She had her head buried into his small chest as she began to rock him back and forth.*

Finally snapping out of it, I ran to his mother's side and couldn't do shit but shake my head. The sound of sirens could be heard nearby but I didn't have it in me to just leave.

"Lege let's go; he dead." again my homie Kill called my name. I looked from Kill to the lady that wouldn't leave her son's side and all I could do was ask for God's forgiveness. Snapping out of it, I ran to my whip and hopped in before I was caught red-handed. I sped off doing nearly 100 mph to leave the scene that I knew would forever haunt me.

1

CHASTITY

5 YEARS LATER....

"I'm really gonna miss you baby."

"I'm gonna miss you too daddy. But don't look like that. I'll be back every break, I promise."

"I know." he faintly smiled. "Now you be good out there Chas. Don't get into no trouble and don't be fooling around with them little knucklehead boys. You focus on your schooling and please don't let that damn Ramera distract you." he added referring to my best friend.

We both had been accepted into Duke University. Since we were kids, this has always been a dream for us. Leaving each other's side would be unheard of because we were stuck like conjoined twins at birth. Duke had been our first choice. Well, it was my choice and Ramera decided to tag along. I had been accepted into Johns Hopkins and a few more schools but I wanted to be with my boyfriend of 2 years. Of course I couldn't tell my father that because he would have a heart attack.

"I'm going to be on my best behavior. I promise I won't let you down. I worked so hard to get here dad. I got this." I smiled to assure him I was gonna make him proud. Hearing me say I worked hard for this made him instantly sad. I could see the embarrassment in his eyes as he dropped his head shamefully.

"Dad, it's okay. I told you. Everything happens for a reason and all you did was made me grind for my education and I made it." again I smiled.

Over the course of time my father had gotten a bad gambling habit and basically blew my college fund my mother had for me stashed away. By the grace of God, I was able to get a scholarship and pay for my education. My father's gambling habit was the only reason I didn't wanna leave because I was too afraid he would gamble off his entire life. His habit was so bad he had gotten fired from his job and lost our home. Thank God he was friends with the previous owner so they showed empathy and rehired him. He was working at a slaughter house where he worked for years but that part of his life he kept away from me. All he ever said was "I kill pigs and cows and package them for shipment." so I never really bothered to ask further.

"YOU GET GOING BABY." My father said knowing it was Ramera knocking at the door.

"Okay. I love you dad." I gave him a great big hug. He helped me to the car with my luggage. He didn't bother speaking to Mera and he moved fast to avoid her. Mera and my dad couldn't stand each other just like Keyon. She couldn't stand my boyfriend and every time they were in each other's presence they argued. "Bye dad." again I hugged him. I hopped into my car and me and Mera pulled off to head to a new journey of life. As much as I was gonna miss my dad I was overly excited to get away from Atlanta. Now don't get me wrong, I loved my hometown and the hospitality everyone had, but I needed something different. So I was off to North Carolina.

∾

2 YEARS LATER...

.   .   .

"HEY CHAS, do you have the notes for Mr. Carter's lectures?"

"Sure Joseph." I reached into my backpack and pulled my notes out. I had studied them so I didn't mind.

"Man you're a lifesaver." he smiled anxiously. Joseph was what people considered a good kid. He got good grades but because he was a workaholic it interfered with his studies.

"Thank you." he stood there with his awkward stare he always gave me. He giggled shyly and began to make small talk. Joseph was really cool. He was the first person that actually introduced himself to me the second day on campus. Keyon hated him and always said he liked me. I would brush it off because I looked at Joseph like a cool homie. He really wasn't my type, not that I had a type, but he wasn't it for me.

"YOU'RE WELCOME JOSEPH." I tried to walk away but he grabbed my arm.

"Umm...so ..umm...where's your bud?"

"She's in her dorm. You like her huh?" I asked laughing.

"No..no..oh no. That girl is a bit too much." he laughed. I couldn't help but laugh with him because Mera was *too much*. She had this hard exterior and didn't care what came out her mouth. She was way too much for Joseph and we both knew it. That girl was a wild one. Since we been here she's been with four boys. She had the nerve to call me corny on a regular basis. She did everything in her power to try and make me leave Keyon but that wasn't happening. I loved Keyon and no matter the rumors around campus I never caught him so I wasn't gonna believe shit she or no one else said.

"Oh boy." Joseph said watching Keyon walk in our direction. "I'll get going." he spoke nervously and scurried off. Keyon walked up and wrapped his arms around me. He was smelling so good I fell into his chest and took in his scent.

"Heyy babyy." I was smiling from ear to ear.

"Man, why that nigga always in yo face?"

"Baby stop. You know damn well I don't want Joseph."

"Yeah aight."

"Yeah aight. Why you looking so good and smelling like that. Boyy..." I smirked and playfully rolling my eyes.

"Girl, you ain't ready." he called me out on my sass. Taking in his words, I paused. Anytime he said this, it would strike a nerve. No I wasn't ready. Mentally, I was scared. I never told Keyon about my past so he didn't understand that I was afraid. So anytime he would make the remark I would turn the other cheek. Right now he was staring me dead in the eyes like he was waiting on my reply. I knew he was tired of waiting and it showed every day.

"I'm ready." my mouth moved but my complete thoughts weren't there.

"What?" he asked astonished. I closed my eyes for a brief second and nodded my head *yes*.

"Hey Chas." I turned around to Mera. "Keyon." she half spoke and rolled her eyes.

"Man I'm talking to my girl; what the fuck you want?"

"I don't want you." again she rolled her eyes. I couldn't do anything but shake my head. This was typical for them. They hated each other so much that I couldn't enjoy the company of my man and friend together. It was always one or the other and the shit was annoying.

"I'mma check you later ma." Keyon reached down and kissed my neck.

"Will I see you tonight?"

"I'm... not sure. I was gonna go hang with the fellas. I'll hit you up."

"Oh okay." I replied sadly. Lately, it feels like things were changing between us. My gut feeling told me it had to do with me not having sex. Just the thought of losing him pained me because he always promised to wait until I was ready.

"Ugh, I don't know why you deal with him?" Mera sassed bringing me from my thoughts.

"Mera, that's been my boyfriend for how long?"

"Yeah, but he's also been here for a year without you. He ain't shit and dun fucked half the girls on campus.

"You don't know that."

"Girl everybody know but you. Stop being so dumb for that nigga. Hang with the fellas my ass. That nigga gonna be at that SLG party tonight. Stop letting him lie so much."

"He doesn't lie to me. He said he's hanging with his boys then he's hanging with his boys.

"Okay so let's bet. Bet $100 dollars he's at that party tonight. We crash it and see for our self."

"Umm...uh...okay." I agreed unsurely. I wasn't the partying type but to make Mera shut the hell up I was willing. She extended her hand out to mines and we shook.

"And if he's not you promise to stop always being so mean?"

"Ugh, I guess."

"Then it's a bet."

As Mera and I headed for my dorm I wanted so bad to tell her what I had told Keyon. She was so judgmental about him that I was second guessing myself. I knew she would probably die but I needed to confide in my friend. It may not be a big deal to others but to me this was a life changing experience.

"I have something I wanna tell you."

"Oh lord." she said and stopped to look at me. I continued to my door and stopped to stick my key into it. Pushing the door open, I frowned because my roommate had left a huge mess.

"Damn, do this bitch ever clean up?" Mera asked stepping over the pile of clothing. Sitting my book bag down, I scooped the clothing up into a pile and took them to the utility room where we stored our washer and dryer.

"That's why the bitch don't clean up because you always do it for her."

"Well if I don't do it, it won't get done."

"You good man." Mera shook her head. She headed into my room and I could hear her flop down on the bed. I headed into the kitchen to grab a bottle of water then joined her in my room.

"So what you wanted to tell me?" she asked as she crossed her legs Indian style.

"Nothing. It wasn't important." I brushed it off because I was unsure if I wanted to tell her. My mind was pretty much made up so I was just gonna tell her after I did it.

"Your mom is so pretty." Mera looked up to the huge portrait of my mom on the wall. looking up at the picture I faintly smiled. I instantly fell into a daze studying my mother's facial features. She was really pretty and everyone that knew her always said I looked like a split image of her. I had her same hazel brown eyes, caramel complexion and small lips. My long, thick and curly hair came from my father along with my button nose.

My mom always showed me pictures of him when he was younger and he had long hair that he always wore in two long braids. My mother always told me stories of my father being a ladies' man and I understood why; he was very handsome and he ran circles around my mother. Her words.

The night my mother was killed I was at my aunt's house spending the night. I would never forget the sound of my aunt's gruesome screams when my father called. She had been murdered in our home and no one knew why. At the time, I was only 9 years old but I had plenty vivid memories of her. That night was the night that my family fell apart. My father went into a depression and began drinking more and gambling away anything of value. I couldn't even grieve because I had to be the strong one for the both of us. When I say my father lost it, he lost it.

As time went by he had gotten better, however, the gambling never stopped. When he gambled off the home my grandmother was raised in, my mother was raised in and she raised me in, I knew then that his habit was bad. I looked over to Mera and smiled. I tried so hard to be thankful for at least making something out of myself. I just wanted to make my mother proud in heaven.

2

LEGEND

"All you do is fuck me and leave."

"What the fuck else I'm supposed to do?"

"Nigga at least take me out. Or how about you make me feel special at least.

"Man you ain't my bitch Karen."

"It's Karlyn."

"Shit, my bad. And that's exactly why; I don't even know yo fucking name yo. Why would you wanna be with a nigga like me ma?"

"Truthfully, I don't know."

"And there you have it." I replied standing to my feet.

I grabbed my keys off the dresser and headed right out ol girl door. The entire way to my whip I shook my head thinking bout the bullshit that had come out her mouth. This chick didn't even know my fucking name. Every time we fucked she screamed out Buck and I tried hard not to laugh. Buck was the alias I told all my hoes because I wasnt telling them my government name. I wasn't the boyfriend type so they didn't need to know shit about me.

"Take me to the slaughter." I spoke into my navigation system.

I bust a U-turn as directed and headed to my place of business.

The Slaughter was my warehouse and aging room that held dozens of animals that we killed and shipped out. Legally, the animals were packaged and shipped but on the illegal side of it, I used the animals to stash and ship my work across the US. The business was left to my pops from my grandpa and I knew my pops was prolly rolling over in his grave knowing what I had turned his business into.

Pulling up to the Slaughter, I hopped out my whip and headed inside. Bypassing my workers I headed towards my top lieutenant and homie Kill office. When I walked in, I instantly knew something was wrong because the nigga was pacing the floor. The minute our eyes locked he gave me this look like whatever it was I was gonna be pissed. I took a seat on the desk to wait for the nigga to speak.

"Man, man, man...you ain't gone believe this shit Lege." he rubbed his hands through his wild curls and looked in my direction.

I didn't bother to speak and he had my full attention. "The shipment that was supposed to go to Honcho is gone.

"Fuck you mean it's gone?" I looked at this nigga like he was crazy.

"Man, I don't know. Shit missing. Every worker is here and counted for except Allen."

"So where the fuck he at?"

"I don't know. The shipment missing and that nigga gone too."

"And you ain't run no tapes?"

"Nah. I just got here and when I asked Calo did the shipment go out he said yeah. I called Honcho just to double check and he said it never made it."

"You gotta be fucking shitting me." I stood to my feet ready to kill every muthafucka in this bitch. Kill was my boy and it wasn't his fault that somebody was being disloyal but this nigga knew how I was when it came to my bread. He was the one in charge of the whole operation but no matter what, I made it my business to check in, and this was the reason I had come here now.

．　．　．

STORMING out the room I headed into the room that was equipped with tons of cameras. Moments later, Kill came in behind me and took a seat in front of the switchboards. Grabbing the remote, he went to the camera that watched the room Allen worked in. I rewinded the tape until he first walked in to begin his shift. After watching the camera for about an hour everything was looking normal.

"Fast forward to about 3 pm." I told him because the shipment was scheduled to go out at 3:30. He forwarded the tape and stopped it right on the beat. Allen had looked at his phone then quickly put it into his pocket. He continued to work until Wayne, one of my drivers, walked in. Allen said something to Wayne and Wayne responded with a nod. Moments later Allen walked away and had left the camera view for about ten minutes.

When he came back into view, he was now changed and wearing the uniforms made for my drivers. The more I watched, the more I begin to grow upset. This nigga had his position for a reason just as Wayne. Wayne was one of my trusted workers which is why I gave him the position of driving. Not having to watch no more I knew exactly what the fuck was going on.

"Get Wayne in here now." I told Kill and took a seat behind the desk. It's like I fell into a daze just thinking bout all the money this nigga was costing me. That truck had a hundred bricks in it which totaled out to $2,000,000. I couldn't wait to get a hold of Allen. When I did this nigga was dead.

THE MINUTE WAYNE walked in the room I whipped out my strap. His eyes grew wide and he clearly knew this shit wasn't good. I fucked with Wayne heavy but if this nigga didn't have my bread he was a dead man. Period.

"You got 2 mill for me?"

"What you mean Legend?"

"I mean 2 million fucking dollars to make up for my fucking truck that's missing."

"I..I..he said he was driving today." Wayne stumbled over his words nervously. From where I sat I could see his hands shaking and his legs looked like they were about to give out.

"And you didn't think to make sure of that? When the fuck have Allen ever drove!?" I jumped into his face.

"I'm sorry man. I didn't..." before he could finish I put my pistol in his mouth. I hated I had to do Wayne like this but this was a irresponsible move. This nigga just not only cost me money, but he cost me a couple bodies because I was gonna go after anything Allen loved.

Pow!

I PULLED the trigger not giving a fuck about all the equipment. Wayne's blood splattered everywhere but I still wasn't satisfied. I looked at Kill and he was lucky he was my boy. My trigga finga was itching to blow this nigga wig back. He looked me in my eyes and I could see his heart beating in his chest. I know he wanted to pull his strap but he knew one wrong move he was dead. We had a stare down for a brief moment until my mind snapped back. I couldn't kill this nigga. This was my boy and we had been through some shit together for years.

"HOLLA AT THAT NIGGA EDDIE. I want this nigga grandma, mama, daddy, granny, kids whoever. I wanna know every fucking move his fam make. Two days." I shot in Kill's direction.

When he nodded his head once, I stormed out the room and headed for the door. I stopped to inform one of my workers about Wayne and instructed him to take Wayne's body to the tunnel to be disposed. I left the building still mad and, after this shit, I just wanted to go home and get my thoughts together. Right now all I saw was red and I was liable to kill anybody. Two mill was a lot of fucking money but it wasn't even that; it was the principle of the matter that this nigga would cross me.

For years, I wanted to get rid of Allen for so many reasons. But out of respect for my pops I kept him around. Him and my dad were cool back in the days. I really didn't know Allen up until he came to work for me. But I had heard nothing but bad shit about him from my pops.

When my pops died, a lawyer got in touch with me and told me I had inherited my father's business and an account with a hunnit bands in it. Imagine my surprise when I walked into a damn slaughterhouse. A part of me wanted to sell it but when I looked at the books, I couldn't believe the amount of money this place made. It's been nearly 8 years since I been running it and everything had been running smooth. With the help from Kill, now deceased Wayne, and my ear on the inside Columbus, shit was easy breezy. Columbus was a FED who I paid good to find out any and everything. Because I didn't move sloppy, I was good on all that wild shit like raids and shit. I was careful who I sold work too and I made sure to never talk drugs on the phone. The phone was the biggest mistake that most d boys had made. Loose lips sink ships and that's what always happened.

3
_____

CHASTITY

"How do this look?"

"It's cool."

"That's what you said about the last three outfits Mera. Damn, you ain't no help."

"Well shit, it's not my fault you tryna get dolled up to get yo feelings hurt. Damn, just throw on something simple."

"Simple. It's jeans and a regular blouse; it's very simple." I replied ignoring the sarcasm about getting my feelings hurt.

"Well you see I'm wearing sweats and a hoodie. But like always yo ass always gotta out-do everybody."

"What the fuck that supposed to mean?" I frowned. "It's not my fault I don't own sweats Mera. And it's not my fault I'm not the type of chick that leave the house in a scarf every morning."

"Whatever." she replied because I had struck a nerve. I swear she bugging.

What I said was true. No I couldn't afford to buy the things I wanted but that didn't mean I had to be a slouch. I didn't have any kids, bills before I got here so what else was my money gonna go on? Unlike Mera, she didn't care how she looked. The same shit she pulled in our neighborhood she pulled here on campus. Who the hell goes outside in a scarf? The shit was just tacky but because I didn't do it I was trying to outshine people.

DECIDING on the jeans and crop, I slid into my white flat boots and grabbed my white bag to match. Just that fast I forgot about the bickering with Mera and focused on the initial plan. We headed out the house for the party. We had a few blocks to walk so we decided not to drive. The entire way, Mera had this weird look on her face I couldn't read. Because she hasn't said much I decided to remain quiet. Every so often I would look in her direction and she had this aggravated look.

She really bugging. I thought shaking my head.

The silent walk to the party was a weird one, and I was happy we were close. From up the street I could see a host of students crowding the front yard, the driveway and the porch was packed. The party was in full swing and the screams that came from the partygoers confirmed that they were intoxicated.

Walking into the home it took forever getting through the crowd. Finally making it in, we could barely see inside. The lights were dimmed, the air was filled with smoke and there was an intense mood because of the R Kelly "Bump & Grind" track that was being played. It looked like a damn freakshow in slow motion. Walking further into the home I began searching for Keyon. And just like I thought he was nowhere in sight.

"Told yo ass he wasn't here." I smirked in Mera's direction. She rolled her eyes and pulled me towards the back of the house. Every door we passed by she opened and we both looked inside one by one. "Mera he is not here. Let's just go."

"We haven't even searched the whole house." she replied and again pulled my arm to guide me.

We headed into the kitchen and when we walked in Jason and Carnell were hugged up with some chicks I had recognized from school. Now this piqued my interest because these were the fellas that Keyon swore he was gonna be hanging with tonight. The minute they noticed us Jason began looking around and that was a dead giveaway.

"Where Keyon at?" Mera asked Carnell.

His eyes wandered towards the outside and before he could lie, I stormed in the direction he was looking. When my feet hit the pavement, my eyes landed right on Keyon. He was leaning on the wall and some chick was all in his face. My blood instantly began boiling but when the girl reached over to kiss him on the lips I lost it. I walked over to where they stood and before I could curse him out, Mera had came from nowhere and began raining blows on the chick. Keyon had realized what was going on so he jumped in between the two and pulled them apart.

"For real Keyon?" I asked him with tears threatening to fall. Mera was cursing him out so bad I couldn't get a word in. That fast she had went ballistic and seemed more upset than me.

"Man, it ain't what you think. This the homegirl."

"Homegirl my ass. The bitch kissed you Keyon!"

"Nigga you ain't shit. I told you Chas this nigga wasn't shit."

"Man, mind yo fucking business." he walked up into Mera's face. "Why the fuck you bring her here anyway."

"She ain't bring me here." I tried to add but failed.

Again Mera and Keyon began to argue and I was growing tired of the both of them. I stormed out of the party and headed for my dorm. The twenty minute walk took me ten I was so angry. When I walked in, I went to my room and buried myself into my pillow. I tried my hardest not to cry but I couldn't help it. I kept picturing the girl kiss Keyon and it was something about it that seemed too comfortable. Keyon wasn't the kissing type so this confirmed they were an item. I began to think of all the rumors I had been hearing and just because of this one incident I was starting to believe they were all true. I couldn't believe that I was so foolish.

"Chastity are you okay?" I heard Nancy's voice and my door creaked. I looked up from my pillow and she stood there with a concerned look. I wanted to lie so bad so she would just leave but the tears were evident I was hurting.

Other than her being a pig, Nancy was really cool. We hung out a lot in our dorm but every time Mera came around she would lock up in her room. She hated Mera and of course Mera hated her. Nancy would always tell me watch Mera and something about her rubbed her wrong but I always let it go over my head. Mera was my girl since kids and we were like Thelma & Louise.

"No." I replied to Nancy and rolled over to face her. I began telling her what happened and she couldn't believe it. She was the one who always took up for Keyon and told me don't listen to Mera nor the rumors. Everything about Nancy was always so positive. She had a great heart and really good spirit.

"So who is the chick?"

"It's Marion friend. She has Mr..." before I could finish the sound of the doorbell alarmed us. Nancy shook her head as she left my room to open the door. Moments later I expected to see Mera but it was Keyon. Rolling my eyes I turned my head because right now I didn't have shit to say to him. He stood there and watched me for a few moments then took a seat on my bed.

"I know I fucked up Chas but you gotta understand that chick don't mean shit to me. I apologize for hurting you but a nigga got needs."

"So you cheated because I ain't having sex?" I turned around to face him. "You promised you'd wait for me Keyon."

"I know but damn ma. It's been years. I got needs shit."

"So all the rumors are true about you sleeping with different women on campus."

"Hell nah. I ain't even touch her. I ain't gone lie either. I was prolly gonna hit tonight. But like I said she don't mean shit to me." he slid over closer to me. When he tried to wrap his arm around me I quickly moved. "Man, come here." he pulled me into his embrace. I was still upset but I felt better he had come to explain himself. "I love you girl. It's time you become a woman and give me what I deserve. I swear if you give me this." he said and swiped his hand across the crotch of my jeans. "I'll be good." he finished.

He moved his head closer to my neck and started placing soft kisses on me. I wanted to tell him stop but it felt too good. He grabbed my hand and put it on his jeans. The bulge in his pants let me know he was rock hard. I closed my eyes as my hand trailed up to his belt. My heart continued to pound and suddenly I stopped myself.

"We can't do this?" I began fidgeting.

"Why, what's wrong? I thought you said you was ready."

"I am ready but I wanted my first time to be special. Candles, wine nice dinner ya know?"

"Yeah I understand. So let's set a date."

"This weekend." I replied nervously. Saturday was two days away but that would give me time to at least go purchase something sexy. I always said the day I lost my virginity would be romantic. Especially because of the way my body was forcefully taken as a child. What I did fail to tell, was, for all those years I was being raped, the attacker never penetrated my vagina. That sick bastard took my anal like it was nothing. He would rape my asshole until I bled remorsefully and this was another reason I was scared.

The sound of Keyon's phone ringing brought me from my thoughts. When he didn't answer I assumed it was the chick calling and I instantly became jealous. The caller called again two more times and he didn't bother to answer neither call. Suddenly my phone rang and when I looked at the caller ID it was Mera. Pushing end on the call I sent her to voicemail and sat my phone on the dresser. I found it odd that the moment Keyon's phone stopped ringing my phone began to ring. I looked at him and he was now reading a text. It was like he could feel me staring because he looked over and had this dumb look on his face.

"Who's that?" I couldn't help it; I just had to know.

"It's Jason." he quickly replied but I could tell he was lying. Leaving it alone I snuggled up under him. I didn't want to ruin the moment because soon we were gonna do something we both had been waiting on for years.

4

LEGEND

"So far, all we have is a daughter. Chastity Roberts, who is currently attending Duke University. Here's a few pictures we have gathered. She's 20 years old, has a boyfriend by the name of Keyon McCoy, always visits Joe's Crab Shack and here is her dorm info, grades GPA and anything associated to her." Eddie slid a folder in front of me.

When I opened it, there were numerous pictures of Allen Robert's daughter. I stared at the pictures for a brief moment taking in her appearance. She looked so sweet and innocent I couldn't do shit but shake my head. Her pops had her caught up in some shit she prolly had no idea about. But in this game, there was no remorse. Nigga didn't have remorse when he took food from my mouth so why the fuck should I show any on his behalf? Now don't get it twisted; It was a possibility she might survive this shit. I needed to use her as my bate in hopes Allen would turn over my shit. I hoped like hell I wouldn't have to kill her but if this nigga didn't cooperate, her blood was on his hands.

. . .

I CONTINUED to shuffle through the pics and the more I went through them the more I shook my head. Her bitch ass boyfriend was living foul and by the smiles she wore on most of the photos she really loved this nigga. I couldn't front if I wanted to. Chastity Roberts was pretty as a muthafucka. Her light brown eyes had a nigga in a daze. She had wild curly hair with the most perfect nose and lips. Everything about her screamed innocent but too bad I was gonna have to kill her.

I PULLED my phone from my pocket and dialed Kill. When he answered I told the nigga pack his bag; we had a trip to take. He already knew what I meant so he agreed and there was nothing else to be said. Tonight we were gonna roll out but first I needed to get my adrenaline pumping. I sent a text to one of my little bitches Stacy to let her know I was on my way to her crib. I then excused Eddie and headed out the door behind him.

As I DROVE through my city, I had my beats up bumping my Nipsey Hussle Marathon CD. The streets were quiet and the moon shined through my front windshield. I had my window slightly cracked taking in the slight breeze that came through. For some reason my mind fell on Arian. I thought back to the day that I fucked up our bond. She had caught a nigga with his pants down literally. Out of all my bitches, Arian was the only one I had love for. We had grew up together and I was the one to even take her virginity.

For years she wanted something I just couldn't give her and that was *commitment*. No matter how much I told myself fuck a bitch, a nigga had major love for her. However, I don't know why I just couldn't settle down. One thing about me, I didn't trust bitches which was foolish because Arian was the type of chick that I could give a hunnit bands to hold and leave for years. When I get back my shit was there and all counted for. Not only that but back in the days she took a case for me and even took the shit to trial. I had the best lawyers on her case and she beat it 12 in the box. No matter how loyal a chick was, I watched the shit my homies had went through with their bitches and baby mamas and I wanted no parts.

After the case Arian had took, I knew I couldn't jeopardize her freedom again. I sold crack for a living and not just crack, but lots of crack. I was the plug in my city but I wasn't no small time hustla. Shit, I sold work to Mexicans and Black men with money. You had to buy at least 20 birds to even do business with me. And if not, then you would have to holla at my boy Shaq who didn't mind running small time shit.

Few years ago, one of my good niggas hit me with a proposition of a lifetime. I was ten bands up but I lost a friend. *Brandon*. I thought and nodded my head. Me and Brandon had been boys for years and I let my dick fuck that up. Three years ago he came at me on some test shit. When he broke the shit down to me, I wanted so bad to object but when he hit me with the ten bands I knew he was on some desperate shit. He had this chick named Bianca that he was gonna propose to, but first he wanted to know if she was loyal. He had me get at her and set her up. I was only supposed to lure her into a hotel and get pictures. Instead my dumbass ended up fucking her. A sudden knock at the door made me think it was Brandon but hell naw; it was Arian. Thanks to *share my location* on iPhone, she came to the room and like I said I was caught with my pants down.

Arian and Bianca were mad cool because of Brandon and I, so this shit hit her in the heart. I felt so guilty that when the time came for me to give Brandon the info I had to confess. I may be a dog but disloyal I wasn't. I gave the nigga back his ten gee's and after the tears he shed I knew our friendship was over. Brandon basically disappeared off the face of the earth but I was reminded by it every day because Arian threw it up in my face every chance she got. Until this day she still wasn't fucking with me but we remained friends. Well, fuck buddies because I still smashed from time to time. No matter what the fuck Arian said, she wasn't going nowhere and if she ever thought she was gonna run off with another nigga then she was gonna be dead along with him. Simple as that.

~

AFTER FUCKING the shit out of Stacy I slapped two bills on her dresser and got ready to head out.

"Thank you." she didn't put up a fight unlike Karen. Stacy knew what it was. We fucked, I broke her off with a few bucks and left. She had some fire ass head that literally took my soul. No lie, she was bad as fuck too. One would think her body was paid for but it was all hers. Unlike her cousin Megan, who was also her roommate, everything that bitch had was bought compliments of AOD strip club.

"Fasho." I told her and let myself out. I walked down the long hall and when I looked back I didn't see Stacy coming behind me so I bent a right into Megan's room. She was sitting on the bed with an attitude, something she did every time I came around. I never understood that shit because Stacy was the reason I met her.

"Man wipe that dumb ass look off yo face. Take that shit off." I told her as I locked the door behind me. She rolled her eyes but her ass still stood up to strip. I peeled out my clothes and when she did the same I shook my head just looking at her fake ass. I couldn't front though; that muthafucka was nice and fat. My dick stood at attention as I watched her walk over to me. Now this what I liked about Megan, she always took the lead. She was a cold freak but that shit didn't work with me. I knew exactly what she was doing; she was trying to make a nigga fall in love. Her pussy was good as fuck but naw, try again hoe. I didn't understand how could a bitch think I would fall in love with her after allowing me to fuck her cousin, who was in the next room, then come in and fuck her. Now Stacy on the other hand didn't know I was knocking Megan down but Megan knew. And the nerve of the bitch to be mad.

I REACHED down into my pants and grabbed a magnum. I rolled it on my dick and slightly leaned on her dresser. "Bust down ma." I told her and she did just that. She stood in front of me, bent over and eased back onto my dick. Her pussy was so damn tight I couldn't understand it. She didn't have any kids but I'd fucked plenty bitches that had kids and still had good pussy. Man I swear this bitch did something to her pussy and it wouldn't have surprised me.

"Ughhhh shit Buck!" she moaned out like I was killing her.

"Man shut yo ass up." I told her as I continued, trying hard not to laugh.

As I continued to slam inside of her, she let out some soft cry like moans. I wanted so bad to yell out "damn this pussy good" but I wasn't the type to talk during sex. To me talking was personal and I didn't get personal with these hoes. So instead I let the sound of my thighs smacking against her ass talk for me. Each time I pulled out the condom was covered with her juices. We had been fucking for at least forty minutes and I didn't wanna cum. Knowing I had business to take care of, I focused on my nut and waited for it to shoot into the condom. Megan had cummed multiple times so my work here was done.

"Buck when you gone finally settle down? I'm ready." my head swooped so fast it damn near broke my neck. This bitch had to be out her fucking mind.

"Man Megan I'm not the nigga for you shorty. I'm a dog ass nigga that's just gonna break yo heart."

"Not if I put this pussy on you every night."

"Pussy! Pussy?" I asked in my best Soulja Boy voice. "I get pussy by the pounds. If you think pussy gone make a nigga wanna be with you then you don't know much. I'm not just talking bout me, I'm speaking for every nigga on earth. Megan stop belittling yourself ma. Now don't get me wrong; you got gold between your legs but it's plenty bitches with that same gold. You gotta do better and expect more. You ain't even got your shit together. You living in the next bitch house. So what would you expect from me? To move you in and rescue you like I'm some captain save a hoe ass nigga. Now you might find one at the club you work at but you got the wrong nigga here shorty."

I grabbed my fitted cap and sat it on top of my head. I knew what I said hurt her but I didn't know how to be nothing else but real. She sat with a dumb look on her face because she knew I was right. Just like I had done Stacy, I went into my pocket and pulled out three bills. I gave her an extra hunnit because her pussy was better. Now most niggas will call me a trick and, guess what, I didn't give a fuck. I did this because couldn't no bitch say they ever gave me shit. Fair exchange wasn't no robbery and especially to a nigga like me. I wiped my ass with three hundred dollars. At only 26 I was a fucking million-aire. See the one thing about me was, I was gonna get it out the mud regardless. My father's business was only a better way to help me transport my work. Even without it, I moved kilos by the day. I had everything made for a young king and didn't owe nobody shit. Yeah I had a few goons but I built my shit on my own. I had a fat crib, 6 whips that cost over a hundred bands for each, no wife, no kids so everything was all mines. So back to the matter at hand, a few bucks wasn't shit. The money I gave Stacy and Megan was gas money.

"You gone call me?" Megan asked bringing me from my thoughts. I shook my head because this bitch knew damn well I wasn't no phone nigga. I nodded my head no because I wasn't gonna lie.

"I might text you aight." I told her and headed for the door. I felt her eyes as they followed me all the way out. I headed out the front door and locked it behind me. I stood on the porch for a few seconds taking in the air because a nigga felt like he just ran a marathon.

WHEN I CLIMBED into my whip I hit Kill to see was he ready. When he replied back *yes* it was time to get in my grimy mode. This was about to be a mission I should have let my team handle but I needed this shit done. You know the saying "if you want something done you gotta do it yourself?" Well this was one of these cases. I couldn't risk someone fucking this up. I needed to get ahold of Allen by any means so I was handling this shit myself. I couldn't wait to get my hands on that pretty little daughter of his. This was my last resort. I had my workers go by this nigga crib, check every hotel in the city and I even had Columbus doing perimeter checks on the highways. It's like this nigga had just vanished.

5

CHASTITY

Looking myself over in my full-length mirror, I was satisfied with the lingerie that Nancy had helped me pick out. I had took her along with me shopping because right now she was the only one I could tell about my night with Keyon. I didn't bother telling Mera because all she would do was talk me out of it so I confided in Nancy instead. Nancy on the other hand was hyped. She gave me pointers on what to do and even helped me decorate our dorm. I had candles set up around my room and even rose petals that she suggested. I decided to skip the candle light dinner because I wanted to get it over with.

"Okay Chas, good luck. I'm gonna stay at Greg's for the night. Now don't forget what I said, be sexy and use condoms." she smiled making me giggle.

"Gotcha. And thank you so much Nancy."

"You're welcome. And stop looking so nervous; you look beautiful." she told me and headed for the door. The minute she stepped out my stomach began doing summersaults. I headed into my room a nervous wreck. I pushed play on my Bluetooth and began to play Fantasia's Pandora station.

. . .

LOOKING over at my alarm clock it was almost time. Keyon said he would be here at 8:00 PM and it was ten until. He lived on the other side of campus but knowing him he would drive. One thing about Keyon he didn't walk anywhere. He was spoiled as hell growing up and Mrs. McCoy had bought him his first car at fifteen. Because Mrs. McCoy watched me grow up she loved the idea of Keyon and I hooking up. Since I been here she would always call to check up on the two of us. Even though she called him she would still ask me questions about how he was doing and his whereabouts. She knew I loved her like a parent but I had got into the habit of lying. Keyon had started slacking in his studies and no matter how much I tried to push him he lacked.

KNOCK! *knock! knock!*

I HEARD the sound of three knocks from in my bedroom. Not wanting to seem so desperate I waited for a few moments for him to knock again. When he did, I let out a deep sigh and headed into the living room. When I pulled the door open Keyon stood there with a smile. I don't know what kind of cologne he was wearing but it tickled my nose alluringly. He was also looking cute in a pair of jeans, a polo shirt and a polo hat to match. He wore a jean jacket and a pair of jean Vans to match his coat.

"Damn." he said eyeing the red lingerie that barely covered my love box.

"You like what you see?" I asked trying to play big girl.

"Hell yeah." he stepped in and closed the door behind himself. He walked up on me and began kissing my neck. I quickly pulled back because I expected to at least chat for a while.

I PULLED Keyon's hand and led him into the room. When we walked in he stopped to look around at all the candles. The look on his face told me no one had ever done this for him. Smiling in the inside just knowing, I took a seat on the bed.

"Sit down; let's talk."

"Talk?" he frowned but he still walked over and sat down.

"You know I love you right Keyon." he nodded his head yes. "Can I ask you a question?"

"Go ahead."

"Are you really still a virgin? I just wanna know because I want us to experience this together."

"Yeah I'm still a virgin. I told you I didn't fuck that girl that night. Shit I came here remember."

"Oh yeah." I replied. It was true he had come here right after the night I caught him. He ended up staying with me until the early morning so there was no way he could have slept with her. We both sat on my bed and a awkward silence filled the air. I was so nervous that I began twirling my thumbs together. When Keyon moved closer to me my heart began to thump.

"Stop being so nervous Chas." he said and grabbed me around my neck. He brought his face into mines and placed a kiss on my lips.

"Okay. But we have to use a condom."

"Don't trip I got you." he chuckled and pulled a lifestyle from his jeans.

"Why are they open?" I asked observing the box. I took them from his hand and when I looked inside there were only two. I pulled them out and held them up waiting for an explanation.

"Jason." he assured me. I nodded my head okay then laid all the way back on my bed. I watched Keyon as he began to undress and I couldn't help but lust over his body. He ran track for the school so not only was his upper torso sexy his legs were nice and firm. When he pulled his polo briefs off, my eyes wandered to his penis that was rock hard. From the few porns I have watched with Nancy his dick didn't look as big as the other men. It looked like the perfect size but no matter the size I knew I would be in pain.

. . .

KEYON WALKED over where I laid and slid me down to the edge of the bed. A few rose petals flew into the air just as a song came on that caught my attention.

HEARD about my past things I used to do
    The games I used to play
    The girls that didn't last
    I know what's on your mind
    You think I'm doing wrong
    Can I say what is real
    You are the only one

IT WAS crazy how all the songs in the world and Jon B *They Don't Know* came on. Keyon had dedicated it to me a year ago when Mera swore she had seen him hugged up with a girl

named Fallen. He had to have remembered because he smiled looking me in my eyes. After taking in the song for a few seconds he continued his mission. He pulled my breasts from my lingerie and took them into his mouth. He sucked them eagerly but he was slightly hurting me. If this was what most people considered foreplay I wasn't a fan. He was biting on my nipples like a teething baby. When he stopped I was nervous and happy at the same time. I knew because he stopped this meant we were on to the next.... He slid the condom onto himself and dropped the wrapper onto the floor. After securing the condom he grabbed my legs and lifted them into the air. He positioned himself at my opening and the minute he went to slide it inside of me...

BOOM!

THE SOUND of my front door crashing in made us both stop and look over. I looked at Keyon in fear because I had no idea what was going on. Suddenly, three men rushed into my room and snatched Keyon off of me. I tried to pull the sheet on top of me to cover my body but I failed because I was snatched up off the bed. I began kicking and screaming for dear life but the shit didn't work. I didn't understand why these men were here. I had never been in trouble in my life so I instantly figured it was something Keyon had done. Before I knew it, one of the men covered my mouth with a brown cloth. I tried hard to fight him off of me but I felt myself getting weaker and weaker as I inhaled. The last thing I saw was Keyon on the ground bleeding then I suddenly blacked out.

TRYING hard to open my eyes my head was pounding and my neck had a horrible crook. I tried to use my hand in hopes to stop my pounding head but my arms were restrained. Alarmed, I began looking around and everything began to come back to me. Last thing I remembered was three men rushing into my home and forcefully restraining me. My eyes began to welled up with tears because I remembered the last vision I had of Keyon. He was on the floor bleeding and he appeared to be knocked out. I instantly began weeping hoping that he hadn't been murdered. With all the movies I had watched I couldn't help but go into a panic. I tried hard to look around the room but because of my tears everything was a blur. I noticed brick walls that looked ancient. There was a small window up high that exposed the outside and it was still dark. The ray of the moon shined through the window giving me a scene of light.

"Keyon!" I began screaming his name with tears pouring from my eyes. "Keyon!" I cried out and I wouldn't stop until he spoke to me. After calling his name three more times the sound of someone clearing their throat could be heard.

"Cha..hemmm...Chas! I'm here." I could hear his voice coming from the left of me but I couldn't see him.

"Where are we; what's going on?"

"I don't know."

"Well you have to get us out of here. Baby please get us out of here." I continued to cry.

"I'm chained up. I'm sorry. I can't move."

"Oh my god." I began sobbing harder. "Who...who...who were those men. Keyon what have you done?"

"I haven't done anything." Just hearing him say those words made me wonder what was going on. I didn't spend my life getting in to trouble, killing, selling drugs, making enemies of any kind so I couldn't understand for the life of me why this was happening to me. I was young, I was innocent and to think my life would be over over something I had no account for was not only skeptical but heartbreaking. I don't know why, but, I didn't believe Keyon. It had to be him, and because he knew how I lived my life he wouldn't tell me. My body became numb and I didn't have a choice. I closed my eyes and began praying to God. Since I could remember, my mom always kept me in the church house and she made me a believer that God answered prayers. Today I was putting my faith in him and I swore if he answered my prayers I'd be in debt with him forever.

Chapter
Legend

I PULLED up to my Slaughter eager as fuck to deal with the situation at hand. I couldn't wait to see the look on Allen's face when I showed him his daughter on facetime. I exited my whip and headed inside. I walked through the main room that held the slaughtered animals and it led to what we called the Black Hole. Upon entering I flicked on the dim light that was along the brick wall. When I first stepped in I could hear chatter from my two prisoners but they got quiet the minute the light came on. I walked over to the rear of the room and grabbed the steel chair that was covered in dust. Walking over to Chastity, I unfolded the chair and took a seat in front of her. She raised her head to look at me and I could literally see the fear in her eyes. We held a short gaze and it took the sound of her boyfriend's voice to grab my and Chastity's attention.

"Man why the fuck we here?" he asked with a fake tough man voice.

"Speak when spoken to bitch before I flat line yo ass right here in front of yo chick."

"Kill me then." he tried to act hard. I pulled my pistol from my waist band and the nigga eyes bucked.

"You sure you want that?" I asked him but he didn't reply. I was gonna kill this bitch ass nigga anyway. I just needed to holla at Chastity first.

"Nooo please." Chastity cried out shaking her head with a petrified look.

"So is it gonna be you or him because one of y'all have to die?" I wasn't gonna kill her. I just needed to see what level of loyalty she was on. Because if she was loyal to this scumbag ass nigga then for sure she wouldn't give up her pops.

"Who it's gonna be pussy?" I stood from my seat and walked over to tough guy. I stood in front of him waiting for him to say *himself* but when this nigga looked over to Chastity I shook my fucking head.

WHAM!

I SLAPPED the nigga so hard with my strap he flew back falling out the chair.

"Just kill me. Please don't take his life." I looked over and couldn't believe her words. No matter how much of a selfish coward this nigga was she was still willing to take her own life for his.

I walked over to her and took a seat in my chair. For a brief moment I watched Chastity because she was enthralling. I couldn't believe a nigga like this had her or even Allen's snake ass birthed her. This nigga Allen was a sorry sack of shit that didn't deserve a chance on earth. Other than the stories I'd hear from my pops, I watched Allen's every move. He was lazy, a slouch, a gamble-holic and he pretty much lost everything he had. I knew Allen's gambling habit was bad but I would have never thought he would have the balls to steal from me. This nigga knew my get down and knew I wasn't remorseful but I guess it didn't matter because he deceived me. One thing I couldn't take from the old man, was, he was a hard worker and could run my company with his eyes closed. And this was the main reason I kept him around.

"CHASTITY, you willing to sacrifice your own life for this nigga?" I looked her in the eyes to read her. This was something I inherited as a child; reading people. I could always read a person by the way their eyes spoke. And right now, it was evident that she would take her own life for his. "This is how it's gonna go. You're gonna get your pops on the phone and we're gonna get him down here."

"Are... are you going to kill him?" she asked with this rattled look on her face.

"I hate to say, but yes. I'm sure you know about your pops' gambling habit." I waited for her to reply but she said nothing. "He stole nearly 2 million dollars from me so he gotta pay. Now you on the other hand, I'll let you live but yo old man gotta go ma." I pulled the phone I had purchased just for this from my pocket and went to hand it to her. She shook her head no stubbornly just as I figured.

"Just kill me. If it's worth the money just kill me." she began crying but she didn't tear her eyes from mines. *This girl serious,* I thought watching her. I lifted up from my seat and wanted so bad to pop her ass but I couldn't bring myself to do it.

Forcefully kicking the empty chair across the room, I watched it crash into the wall. This was something I did when I was upset. I would tear shit up and I remembered times when my mother had to restrain me to keep me from destroying our home. Cuffing my temple into my hand I tried hard to control the angry I felt rising. I did what I always did when I was upset and that was count and take deep breaths.

I walked back over to Chastity and tried to hand her my phone again. But again she denied me. Tired of playing games with her, I stepped over to her precious little boyfriend and aimed my gun at his head. I looked over to Chastity and this was a decision she would have to make. It was saving Keyon or calling her father. When she didn't speak, I took it as she was calling my bluff so I squeezed my trigger and sent six bullets into his body killing him instantly.

"Noooooo! Keyon! Oh my godddd!" she screamed in a loud shrieking voice. "Oh my godddd! You're a monster! You're a murderer! You're a child killer!" she continued to bluntly assault me. The last statement she said caught me off guard. I shot her a look of guilt and it's like my past had begun to replay in my mind. I stood frozen for what seemed like an eternity until I finally snapped back to reality. I pulled my phone from my pocket and began to record her screams. I shot Chastity one last look then headed for the door. The sound of her sobs was doing something to me so I left the Black Hole with my mental fucked all up. I needed to get away from this girl and fast. Her words were to unbearable. *Yes* I was a killer but that child killer part stung hard. Shit sent a chill through my body that was disturbing. I knew this was gonna be a long, fucked up night for me so I was gonna clutch of bottle of cognac to numb me.

WHEN I MADE IT UPSTAIRS, I hit who I referred to as The Corner. It was two men that worked in the warehouse and not only did they dispose animals, but they got rid of bodies for me as well. A part of me wanted to leave her boyfriend laying there so she could realize this shit wasn't a game. But because of all the illegal shit I had going on, I couldn't take the chance. Now drugs I could handle but a nigga wasn't about to be sitting in jail fighting murders and shit. Especially how the media would play it out. Young college boy with a future ahead of himself murdered by a child murderer. I shook my head at just the thoughts and made my way to my whip.

Right now I was in a zone so home wasn't where I wanted to be. Fuck it, I decided to head out to AOD's and have a drink. I needed to figure this shit out with Chastity. I knew after what I had done, I was gonna have to kill her as well. She would for sure go to the police on a nigga and I couldn't take any chances. However, first I had to lure this nigga Allen in. I pulled my phone from my pocket and went to Allen's number. The nigga's voicemail had been picking up but if he checked it, he would for sure hear the screams of his daughter.

"YOU WANT A DANCE?"

"Bitch, do it look like I want a dance?" I mugged a stripper by the name of Cinnamon. Rolling her eyes she stormed away from my section. I watched her as she headed up the red carpet and right up to another man that sat with his dollars out and ready. Taking a sip from my cup I began fondling with the buttons on my phone. I had received a few texts from Kill but right now I wanted to be left alone. I decided to call him once I left when I was good and drunk and my mental was back in check. It wasn't nothing personal about Kill he was my boy and had been for years. We hustle together and just because the empire was mines I made sure to look out for him as an equal. I wasn't the type of nigga that felt I didn't need an army. True I could run shit alone but with the work Kill, Shaq, Wayne and even Allen had put in, my shit was solid. Now Wayne and Allen were a different breed of Kill and Shaq. These niggas were my boys and Allen and Wayne were just workers.

Kill and I were the closest out us three. Shaq became my boy on the strength of Kill and at the time we were all kids. After a few obstacles, Shaq had proved himself so I took a liking to him. These niggas had been around since I stole my first bag of chips from the corner bodega. They were around when I stole my first bike out some Hispanic man yard and literally had a shootout. These niggas had even been there to console me when my pops broke the news to me that my mother was dead. At the time I was only 11 years old and the first mention of it didn't hit me at that very moment. It was the news segments that were plastered across the news that disturbed me. It's like the shit came on so much I was afraid to watch television. I couldn't sleep at night and with my pops always at work I would just go to Kill's crib and crash.

The situation with my mother not only affected my heart, but it also fucked with my ego. For years, I was getting clowned in school when people found out who my mother was. To the world and media, she was a whore that had been raped. But that wasn't the case. My mother was a stripper that provided for me by any means. At the time, my father's company didn't make the money we make now because he ran his shit legally. Therefore, my moms stepped up to the plate and did what she had to do to make ends meet.

On one late night she was leaving the club and was followed home. At the time her car was fucked up so she caught a local bus. The man she worked for name Larry was lenient so he gave her a early shift which was 4 PM to 9 PM so she wouldn't be out late but that shit didn't matter. 9:56 PM my mother was pronounced dead. Cause of death was strangulation. She had been raped and murdered by the hands of a man that was known around the world now as The Grim Ravisher.

Years after my mother's death, two more strippers had been killed and murdered the same way forcing Larry to close his club. As years went by, nearly a dozen women had been murdered and they connected all the murderers to the man that had killed my moms. Until this day, there was no signs of him and nothing that led to him because of a mask he wore. So every murder was basically archived. As years went by, I finally found the strength to put my mother's death behind me. I don't know why but in my heart I knew I would avenge her death. And really I didn't give a fuck if they locked me away for the rest of my life. Even behind bars I would get the sense of peace I needed.

· · ·

"HEY BUCK." a soft voice spoke my name bringing me from a cold daze. I knew who the voice belonged to so I didn't wanna look up.

"Sup Megan." I took a sip from my drink and tried to ignore her.

"Surprised to see you here. My shift almost over; can I roll with you tonight?"

"Nah I'm cool. I just came to have a drink. I got business to handle."

"Oh okay." she said with the same pout face she always wore. I was starting to grow impatient with this chick. It was beginning to show that she was catching feelings for me and that couldn't happen. The only chick I had feelings for was Arian and if I didn't die with her as my wife, couldn't no bitch get a title out of me. Period.

6

LEGEND

After two days of waiting on Allen's call the nigga hadn't bothered to reach out. I knew he was a heartless bastard but I was sure he hadn't checked the message. I had a feeling he would leave Chastity for dead however, I hoped he wouldn't. For years Allen always spoke of a daughter and when he did his eyes would glow. I didn't spend much time around him to find out every detail about her but I knew he loved her. Every detail I had of Chastity was from Eddie who had followed her every move. I knew she liked Daisies from the decor in her bedroom. I also knew she liked seafood because she had visited Joe's Crab Shack on numerous occasions.

When I told this nigga to find out every detail he went to the extreme. The nigga even had her favorite song documented which was Ashanti "Baby". I don't know why but all this shit was in my mental bank. For some strange reason she was on my mental heavy. I hadn't seen her since the day I murked her nigga but today was the day to face her. I knew by now she was starving because it's been three nights since she's been in the Hole. I had Kemp my chef hook her up something so right now I was on my way down to feed her.

. . .

As I MADE my way towards the Black Hole, my heart thumbed in my chest for no apparent reason. I took the two steps that led into the hole and hit the light. Just as I figured she was balled up in a fetal position and the sound of her weeps echoed through the room. Walking further towards her, I bent down and tugged at the chains that were securely wrapped around her arms. Instead of the normal fearful look, she wore this look of pure disgust. Ignoring her I cuffed her hands but I left her ankle chained up to the longer chain that would make it more comfortable for her to move around. It didn't reach the door but it was long enough for her to lay on the small cot that sat in the corner. There was a blanket along with a pillow to make her stay more comfortable.

"Here I brought you something to eat. And in that bag is something for you to put on." I pointed towards the duffle bag that contained a pair of my sweats and a shirt. By the way her body shivered I knew she was cold. She was still wearing some bullshit red lingerie that she thought was sexy. Just looking over her body my insides boiled thinking bout the day we had ran up in her crib. I visualized her on the bed with ol boy wrapped in between her legs. I shook my head just thinking about it. I guess I was mad she was so loyal to a nigga that didn't mean her no good. I could tell Chastity was a real naive chick and it disgusted me.

FOR A SPLIT second I stood here and watched her until the sound of her cough brought me too. "Man put them clothes on." I told her because it was evident she was getting sick. She didn't reply to me so I walked away from her to let her eat. I headed out the room and made sure to lock the door behind me. I headed up to my office and took a seat behind the cameras. I zoomed into the camera that was in the room with Chastity and fell into a daze watching her. She was still crying and hadn't even bothered to grab the bag of food nore the clothing. Got damn Taurus, I thought knowing she was stubborn as hell.

. . .

"WHAT'S UP LEGE." I looked over to Kill's voice. He walked into the room and took a seat to join me. I was so in tune with watching Chastity that it made him focus in. We both watched her and neither of us said a word. Finally breaking my concentration Kill looked over at me.

"So what we gone do with her? Shit we can't keep her alive."

"We not killing her." I replied without looking his way.

"So what we gone do with her?"

"Shit I'mma hold her until this nigga answer his phone. I'm sure the nigga ain't gone just leave her for dead."

"And if he do?"

"He not." I shot finally looking over at him. I was confident Allen had some type of heart. Shit Chastity was a pleasant and gentle creature that God had blessed him with. Going over the forms from Eddie she always smiled. Her grades were A1 and she seemed to not bother a soul. How could a man just abandon that? Therefore what Kill had to say didn't matter.

"Well I just hope you're right because we both know Allen and he don't give a fuck about nothing but a poker table. Clearly he don't give a fuck about his life because if he did he wouldn't have stole all our shit."

"Just because he don't care about himself don't mean he don't care bout his seed."

"You right." Kill said agreeing with me.

He had kids so he understood the love for a child. I didn't have kids but the love my mom and pops showed me was the world to me. How can someone not love their kids? When my moms was murdered it was just me and my pops for years. He died when I was almost 18 years old. He had a stroke that had fucked him up badly. He was hospitalized then sent home after 8 months. Four years later, he had another one that killed him. His brain didn't receive enough oxygen or nutrients so it caused his brain cells to die. Because he was sick for so many years I copped with the fact he would be dying soon. So it didn't come as a shock; it actually mentally prepared me.

. . .

TAKING my eyes off Kill I watched as Chastity laid back on the cot. She still hasn't touched her food and I swear I wanted to go down there and beat her ass. Like I always did, I shook my head at the thought of her basically giving up. It's been days since she ate so to me she was just giving up. I bit down on my jaw just thinking about her giving up over that pussy ass nigga. She was in love with him and it showed every day.

~

CHASTITY

I LAID on the cot and couldn't do anything but cry. The thought of those bullets piercing though Keyon's body was disturbing. I was cold, I was hungry, I was heartbroken and most of all I was afraid. I knew that only a matter of time I was next and to be honest I didn't care. Just watching Keyon's lifeless body made me wanna give up. The love of my life was dead and I knew sooner or later my father would be joining him, so what else was there for me to live for. It was something about the Killer's eyes that told me he wanted my father and bad. And I know I pissed him off by not calling but I couldn't.

MY EYES ROAMED over to the bag of food but because I was so rattled I couldn't even eat. It had sat there for two days and I was sure it had spoiled. Truthfully, I didn't care because I was gone starve myself to death, that's if they didn't come in to kill me first.

I was in a damn dungeon that looked deserted and in the middle of nowhere. The only reason I knew there was life outside of the room was because the smell of blood and meat that seeped from underneath the door. There was a metal door on the opposite wall but no handle to open it. Not knowing what these men were capable of I could have possibly been in a damn warehouse where they stored bodies. This was another reason I couldn't eat. The smell turned my stomach upside down along with the visions I had of Keyon's blood. I couldn't get the pictures of his lifeless body out my head no matter how much I tried.

I never thought in a million years that I would experience something as tainting other than my rape. Well I was wrong. I had never in my life saw a real dead body other than the horror movies I had watched. And it pained me more that the body belonged to the only man I ever loved other than my father.

THE SOUND of the door creaking made me inhale and my sudden heart beat began to increase. The dim light came on and without looking in his direction the scent of his cologne filled the air. *Who the fuck wears cologne when they're gonna kill* I thought trying hard to think of something to make my nervousness ease down a bit. It may sound crazy but every day I was in this room I tried hard to prepare myself for death.

The sound of his footsteps coming closer to the cot made my body tremble harder than I was. I tried to lay still in hopes he'd think I was already dead but I was sure he saw the quiver from my body. He didn't say a word but I could feel his presence. Not only that but his cologne had become stronger making me sniff softly. Hell I was tired of the smell of raw meat or dead people.

"So you ain't gone eat?" his voice echoed around the empty room. I tried hard to ignore him until he used his foot to kick me in the ankle. Finally turning my head to face him, I looked him in the eyes but I remained silent. Tonight he wasn't wearing a baseball cap so his deep jet black waves were exposed. For the first time I actually got a good look at his face; boy was this man handsome. Who would think a man as gorgeous as him would be so heartless. My eyes scanned his entire appearance and he wore a black tee that did him no justice. He looked like he spent many days in the gym other than just killing people. One look at him you wouldn't think he was a killer until you looked him in the eyes. He had these cold pair of black eyes that held no justification or remorse.

"So you gone just starve yourself to death?" My face frowned with irritation because this nigga had his fucking nerves.

"Shit you gone kill me anyway." I finally replied and turned my head back around to face the brick wall.

I closed my eyes knowing that any minute he would put his gun to the back of my head and just blow my brains out and I was ready. The room fell silent for a split second but I could still feel his presence. Moments later, I heard the door slam and I didn't bother to look up. His scent had disappeared so I knew he was gone. I let out the breath of air I had been holding as I looked towards the floor. The bag of food that was here for a couple days was now replaced with KFC. Just the smell of the chicken made my stomach growl but again I refused. I wanted so bad to at least grab the bag of clothes but I didn't want to give him the satisfaction. Instead I tossed the blanket back over my body and began to cry until my head began to spin and I fell asleep.

TWO DAYS AFTER....

IT WAS NOW day seven that I was still alive and laying on the same dumb ass cot. My back hurt along with my stomach. This morning I had thrown up from hunger or at least I gagged because since I didn't have anything on my stomach nothing came up but my lining. Thanks to the t-shirt he had brought I was able to clean it up. I tossed the dirty shirt along with the bag of food he had brought two days ago to the corner of the room. Finally today I was beginning to regret not putting the clothes on but what good would it do without a shower. I was musty, my vagina hair had begun to grow back so I could smell the must coming from down there.

Looking up at the window I could tell it was morning by the way the air looked and the slight sun that was peeking through the clouds. The small window was the only sense of peace I had but I still couldn't stop the rapid tears that fell down my face. I could feel the puffiness under my eyes from crying so much that it caused my face to hurt. I cried myself to sleep, woke up crying and through the day when I laid here and couldn't sleep I cried. I knew by now Nancy was worried about me and possibly went to the authorities. It was evident something was wrong because of the door that was off the hinges and my phone going to voicemail.

Letting out a deep sigh I stood to my feet to stretch. My legs had went to sleep causing my knees to buckle. I began to walk around the room as far as the chain would let me which wasn't far. The sound of the creaking door made me freeze. I wanted so bad to hurry and run back to the cot but he had already walked in. Our eyes met and held each other's gaze for a slight second. His eyes began to roam my body making me feel uneasy. I was still half naked in the same funky lingerie from the night I thought would be a romantic one. My eyes roamed to the bag he was holding and in an instant my mouth began to water. He was holding a bag from Joe's Crab Shack and the smell of butter garlic crab legs made my stomach growl loudly.

Stubbornly, I walked over towards the cot. No matter what the hell was in that bag I wasn't giving in. When he walked over by me he placed the food on the ground. I looked from the bag to him and I don't know what came over me but I used all the strength I had and kicked the bag across the room. I shot him a challenging look and I swear his eyes went black like they did the night he killed Keyon. I thought for sure he would hall off and punch me, but instead he began breathing hard and counting to himself. It's like he was on a whole other level of psycho.

After he counted to three, he threw whatever he was holding hitting me in the face. He stormed out of the room and slammed the door behind himself. Curiously, I picked up what appeared to be pictures and began grabbing one at a time. Looking over the pictures my heart began to cringe and I could feel the pain and agony build inside of me. Not believing my eyes, I picked up another picture followed by another and each picture broke my heart piece by piece. One picture was of Keyon inside of his car and Mera sat on the side of him. Another picture was of him and Mera coming out of a restaurant holding hands. The next one was of them again in his car kissing. The hurt that I felt was being replaced with anger. All along my best friend had been sleeping with my boyfriend. Everything had begun to play in my mind and I was beginning to piece things together.

The night I caught him with the chick, Mera seemed more upset than me. For some reason she was eager as hell for us to go to that party and especially her confidence in that bet. After, while he was in my dorm, his phone wouldn't stop ringing and right after, my phone rang and it was her. I tossed the pictures around the room furiously as I thought of Nancy's words. *I don't trust her.* Not only Nancy but my dad couldn't stand her either. Tears began to fall from my eyes but I didn't feel that same hurt I felt prior to seeing the photos. I cried out of anger and knowing I wouldn't get the chance to whoop her ass. God as my witness, if I made it out alive I was gonna beat the hoe out that bitch.

I slid down to the ground falling on top of the numerous pictures. I looked around at the scattered photos and couldn't believe it. There had to be at least two dozen. Different days, different scenery and even different ones of them cuddled in his car. There was one picture that stood out the most. I picked it up and looked over my pink shorts and pink halter top. That same day Mera wore the same outfit in yellow and she wore this same outfit in a picture with Keyon. I thought back to that day and pictured it as if it was yesterday. She was supposed to come to the gym with me but made up some bullshit about not feeling good. The numbers on the photo displayed the time and date and it matched perfectly. On the photo it read 10:19 am and my gym sessions were always at 9 AM. I shook my head repeatedly as a fresh set of tears began to run down my face. All along I had been getting played. They smiled in my face and swore they couldn't stand each other and now I understood why.

7

LEGEND

I swear it took everything in me not to beat the shit out of Chas. I legit had to demonstrate my breathing technique so I don't draw down and kill her. I couldn't say I didn't blame her but fuck that, I went out my way to get her something to eat. I literally went to buy her favorite food and for what? For her to throw it across the room. When I made it up to the security room, I began to watch her on the cameras like I did daily. This shit was crazy. It's like I had become obsessed with watching her on the screen. I was visiting the Slaughter more than I ever have. I just hoped like hell no one took notice.

Right now she sat Indian style going through the pictures I had threw in her face. Her hands were shaking and tears spilled from her eyes like a leaking faucet. I knew she was gonna be hurt but she needed to see the shit for herself. Like I said before a nigga like Keyon didn't deserve her. The whole time, he was fucking on her friend right behind her back. Shit, keep it real, it was right in her face. They paraded around town like an item then would go smile in her face like nothing ever happened.

Staring at the screen she didn't look like the broken girl from yesterday. Right now she looked more enraged. After closely studying each picture she finally dropped them and went to sit on the cot. She sat there for a few seconds, and I could tell she was contemplating something. Moments later, she lifted from the cot and grabbed the bag of food. She tossed the plastic bag to the side and began tearing into the brown paper bag. She then took a seat on the cot and started eating the food like a starving child. I watched her as she broke into each crab leg and dipped it into the small black container of butter. *This girl need a shower.* I thought wondering what was I gonna do. I couldn't take her to my crib so the only option was to get a hotel or let her shower here in the Slaughter. *Fuck it.* I thought standing to my feet. I wasn't gonna chance a hotel in case she tried some weird shit.

I HEADED out of the security room and swung by the vending machine to grab Chastity something to drink. I then headed into the lockers to see if I could find a nice clean shirt; thanks to her dumb ass she used the shirt I brought her to clean up spit. By the time I made it to the black hole I had come up on a pair of sweats from Marciella the cleaning lady's locker, along with a pair of socks and a pink shirt. I pushed open the door and stepped inside the room. I walked over to Chas and handed her the Coca-Cola and she had the nerve to look at it like I was trying to poison her.

"I don't drink soda." her big brown eyes looked up at me.

"So yo ass can die of thirst then." she looked from me to the soda and I could tell her ass was thirsty. She quickly grabbed it, cracked it open and began to guzzle it damn near killing it in one swallow. She sat the can down beside her and began twirling her thumbs. After studying her for so long, I knew this was something she did when she was nervous or wanted to ask a question.

"Umm...uhh..can...can I please take a shower?" she asked with her head held down.

"Let's go."

She quickly looked up like she couldn't believe I had told her to come. I mean, I know she was caught up over the fact that she was here but damn I wasn't a fucked up nigga. Shit, I tried to make sure she ate everyday but she decided to starve herself and that was her problem. "Let's go before I change my mind." I unlocked the chain around her ankle. I grabbed her arm and walked her towards the door. "Don't try no stupid shit because you won't make it out alive." I reminded her as I shoved her out the door.

WHEN WE MADE it to the locker room, I demanded everyone to exit. They hurried out the room and I instructed Chastity on the shower she would be using. I needed her close to the door so I can stand here and watch her. Turning on the hot water she looked relieved to finally feel the warmth of water. After running her water, she peered up at me with a confused look.

"So are you gone just stand there and watch me?" she sassed like she wasn't already naked.

"It ain't like you ain't already naked. Look what the fuck you wearing yo." I reminded. She looked down at her lingerie and I could see the embarrassment all over her face.

FINALLY PEELING OUT HER LINGERIE, I could tell she was ashamed of her body. I slightly turned to give her some privacy but I made sure to catch a glimpse. Chastity wasn't all extra thick with a fat ass. She had a small frame standing about 5'4 with a nice little ass that matched perfectly. Her skin was like the color of caramel candy melting inside a rod iron pan. Although she didn't have a big ass and a enormous set of titties she was perfect. She had a pretty face with the most innocent fucking eyes. The way she was moaning right now because of the soothing water had a nigga dick hard as Chinese algebra.

"Damn, can you hear?" she asked making me turn around.

"Sup?"

"Can I get a towel to soap up?"

"Aight hold up." I replied then headed out.

"Jose, watch her." I used my fingers for gestures because the nigga barely spoke English. I ran into our laundry facility where we kept towels, cleaning contents and things like mops, brooms and dust-pans. I grabbed the neatly folded towels and headed back towards she shower.

WHEN I WALKED IN, I didn't see Jose but Chastity was looking directly at me. She had this look in her eyes like she was afraid and some-thing wasn't right about her frown. I stepped closer to her, and now I saw what had her so disturbed. Jose had his back against the wall leaning back on the showers that were across from the one Chas stood in. This nigga had his dick in his hand and was pulling on it like his life depended on it. It was like he didn't give a fuck I was right here because the nigga had not looked my way. The beads of sweat that formed on his forehead and the way his face frowned let me know he was on the verge of busting a good ass nut.

Instantly, my adrenaline began to rush and my eyes went black. I whipped out my strap and fired two shots into his nut sack then one in his head. His body slid down the cold steel wall, and his blood began to flow down the drain and into the pipes. A few of my staff members rushed into the room because they heard the shots but they knew not to say a word. My staff knew what type of nigga I was and the way I paid, them their loyalty was carved in stone.

"Put your clothes on." I told Chastity who stood froze with tears running down her face. I knew what she was thinking; I'm a killer but right now that shit didn't matter. Flashes of my mother's murder had took me into that place so seeing this nigga on some perverted shit caused my blood to rise.

I WALKED to the doorway of the locker room and sent the text to The Corner who I knew was only one room away. I waited for Chastity to finish dressing then took her back into the Black Hole. When we walked in, she headed over to the cot and just like she always did she laid down. That same fear she wore the night I killed her nigga was written all over her face so I pulled the chair up and placed it right in front of her. For a moment I watched her not knowing what to say. Shit, she was still my prisoner but for some reason I was drawn to her. It was some shit I couldn't even explain and I knew she wouldn't understand it.

"Look you need to holla at yo pops so this shit can be over with. You got a nigga in here killing shit behind you and got you thinking I'm a monster. I don't think you realize that all this bloodshed is on your hands Chas. Yo little boyfriend, that's on you. This nigga I just had to kill, on you too. All this shit can be over if I get my shit back." Even though I was still furious I spoke to her in a calm and balanced tone. Like always, her head hung low and she twirled her thumbs in circular motions.

"You think I wanna see this shit? You think I can stand the sight of you killing people in front of me. I don't know what misconception you have of me but I'm not a murderer. I haven't even seen a dead body in my life." Her voiced cracked letting me know she was about to cry. She tried hard to hold back and to my surprise she made eye contact with me. "My father is all I have. Now I wasn't raised in the *hood*, but I know loyalty comes first. I'm not calling my father and if taking my life means that much to you then so be it."

She began furiously fondling the blanket that she picked up from the cot. "I don't give a fuck. My fucking back hurt and I'm tired of sleeping in some blood-smelling fucking dungeon." She pulled the blanket slightly on her body as if she was dismissing me.

In a whole other event or setting, Chastity would have been laying in her own pool of blood. But right now, that wasn't the case. I respected her loyalty to her father because had it been me, I'd feel the same way. Not only that, she seemed like the timid young girl who wasn't raised in the hood but she had heart. I killed two people in front of her so she knew I wasn't playing, however, she still held her ground.

8

CHASTITY

As I fluffed the bullcrap pillow so I can lay down, I could feel whoever the hell he is burning a hole through me. I had really grown impatient with him. I was tired of being in this hell of a hole and not only that, I was tired of seeing bodies dropping like he got paid to do it. This was the shit that Mera always bragged about but to me it was senseless. She was fascinated with hood niggas, something my mother didn't prepare me for. However, it was something about this man that seemed different.

Although his intentions were to kill me, he continued to go out his way for me. When he brought me the Joe's Crab shack that shit blew me back. Joe's was my favorite food and something told me that it wasn't a coincidence. The way he looked at me even piqued my interest because he didn't give me that killer vibe. Before he pulled the trigger, he looked at his prey with hatred through those cold eyes. But when he looked at me, it's like he held some sort of empathy. The way his eyes flipped when he saw that man fondling himself was beyond me. He could have let him just rape me but instead he defended me.

When he left me there with that man alone, it was something about the way he looked at me that made me cringe inside. The moment he unzipped his pants fear took over me because of my past. Then suddenly here comes my knight and shining armor slash killer to save the day. This man was really confusing the hell out of me. It's like he wanted me dead but he went out his way to protect me. However, I wasn't no fool. I knew he was only protecting me because he needed to lure my father in which is why I was still alive.

"GET UP." he spoke just above a whisper but I could still hear the authority in his voice. Sighing out in frustration, I reluctantly lifted from the cot. I walked over and stood in front of him sarcastically with my hands on my hips. His eyes roamed my body instantly making me discomfited.

"Why'd you tell me get up?" I quickly spoke to shift the attention from his stare down. He looked up at me and it's like he began to rethink whatever he wanted. After a faint pause, he stood to his feet and let out soft sigh shaking his head.

"Put yo shoes on and let's roll." he spoke and walked over to the door.

As I slid into my shoes, I said a prayer to myself that we were going anywhere but into the warehouse because it stunk horribly. The entire way to the shower I wanted so bad to gag. I didn't understand how everyone could even take the smell.

As WE WALKED through the warehouse, I observed the room we had walked through to get to the front of the huge building. There were dead animals that hung on ropes making my stomach turn. The men that were aligned behind the tables didn't seem to mind the smell nor the fact they had to butcher the animals. Putting the pieces together, I realized that this was where my father always referred to as a slaughterhouse. It was now evident that my father worked for him which is how he was able to steal from him.

I also observed how the men looked at him as he walked through. It was like everyone feared his presence alone. Another thing I took notice to was, the fact that everyone turned the other cheek of my being here. I mean, did these people not know I was kidnapped or did they not care? Not only Keyon, but also the man he had murdered was done right here in this warehouse full of people. How could they not know?

As we exited the building, I stopped to take in the fresh air. It had been a entire week since I'd seen the outside world. I began looking around to see if I could make a dash for it but I wouldn't make it far. The building was in a secluded area and the many cars that were parked outside I was sure belonged to the staff. He led us to his vehicle which was a candy apple red McLaren 650S. I made a mental note of every detail just in case I needed to give a description of the vehicle. We climbed inside and before we pulled off he reached over to the glove box and pulled out a black bandana.

"Put this on." he said throwing it into my lap.

I took the bandana and tied it securely around my eyes. The sound of his motor roared and seconds later I could feel the vibration from his music. I laid my head back as the car pulled out slowly. Within seconds I could feel the car speed up and my body jerked so hard I knew if I wasn't wearing my seatbelt I would have went flying through the window.

"Aye!" I felt a nudge to the arm and my eyes shot open. I was still wearing the blindfold so I couldn't see anything. We had been driving so long I dozed off during the ride.

The car fell silent then the sound of his car door slamming shut let me know he had got out. Remaining still, I waited for him to give me instructions. When my door opened, he grabbed me around the arm to help me out.

"I'ma take this blindfold off you. Now when we get in here yo ass bet not say shit. And if you try some funny shit, I'mma shoot you." he spoke bluntly. *This nigga just love shooting people.* I thought as I felt him tugging on the back of the bandana. I sighed in relief when the bandana was removed from my eyes because the shit was irritating as hell. Looking around I took notice we were at the Renaissance Hotel. Where? I didn't know but at least I was able to see the name. The moment I got a chance I was gonna call Nancy and tell her where I was at in hopes she'd send the police.

WALKING INTO THE HOTEL, we hopped onto the elevator and took it up to the 8th floor. We stepped off and walked to room 805. He used the key card he held in his hand and opened the door. When we stepped inside, I took a seat in the chair that sat by the window. I looked out into the day's sun and fell into a daze until he called out to me making me look over.

"Look, you gone stay here for a couple days until I figure this shit out. Right now I got my team on a man hunt for yo pops and when I find him you free to go." I watched him as he spoke. I couldn't believe he had the audacity to say it as if I was supposed to say "oh okay, well thank you." I shook my head because this nigga was out of his mind. I didn't understand why he just didn't kill me and let my father be.

"And what happens if you never find him?"

He looked away from me as if he was contemplating his response. There was a faint pause then he looked over to me.

"Then you gone work off his debt." Again he spoke like this shit didn't bother him. Fear began to take over me because how in the fuck was I gonna work off 2 million dollars. The first thing came to mind was him trafficking my body. My eyes began to weld with tears and without force they began to fall. He looked at me again but this time his eyes held repentant.

WITH NOTHING LEFT TO SAY, he walked away from me and headed into the restroom. My eyes roamed over to the door then back towards the restroom. I bit into my bottom lip contemplating making a dash for it. I pictured the outside and thought of the long hallway I would have to run down. I would have to either find the stairs or if luck was on my side the elevator would be open. Knowing how treacherous this guy was, screaming for help wouldn't probably work. I was sure he would kill me and whoever else stood in his way.

Seconds later, he emerged from the restroom and laid on the bed. I watched him as he picked up the remote like it was nothing. He began flicking through the channels and stopped on *Marriage Boot Camp.*

Oh, what the hell. I thought getting up to join him on the bed. I was so afraid that I didn't know if I could get comfortable or not. Then I remembered him saying I would be staying here for a few days. Now what I was puzzled about, was, would he be staying with me? I was more than sure he wouldn't leave me alone. Back at the dungeon, I was always locked away. No matter how much he went out his way, I was certain he didn't trust me enough to leave me alone. Letting out a sigh, I fluffed my pillow and laid back. He picked up the remote and turned from my show. I wanted to tell him turn it back but I knew that would be pushing it. Zooming into the screen something more interesting than *Marriage Bootcamp* caught my attention. It was the news and it showed my campus.

"I'M KATHERYN COSTA, here live at Duke University, where two teenagers have gone missing. One of the students that is the roommate of one of the missing students have filed the missing person report. Missing, is, 20 year old Chastity Roberts and 21 year old Keyon McCoy. Here with me are the best friend and roommate of Roberts."

MERA AND NANCY appeared on the screen both crying hysterically. Nancy, who looked sincere, made my eyes welled up with tears. Mera, on the other hand, looked like she was forcing herself to cry.

"CHAS, if you see this please call me. I'm really worried about you and

Keyon. Please come home." Mera spoke making my jaw clench. She wasn't worried about me. She was more worried bout Keyon and it was evident.

"We've spoken to the parents of McCoy and they are very concerned. If you have any information please contact the NC police department. Back to you in the studios Montell."

I TURNED AWAY from the television and began aggressively fluffing my pillow. This was another thing I did when I was annoyed or frustrated. I laid my head down and turned away from *him*. After seeing this shit, I was bothered. I wondered if any of this had any type of effect on his heart. From what I've seen he was heartless but damn. I didn't have shit to do with my father's half-witted behavior.

"How long you and ol girl been friends?"

I didn't say anything for a few seconds because I was busy now crying. After a few sniffles, I was able to balance my voice and respond.

"Since we were young." Visions of Mera and I as kids began to play in my mind. I couldn't believe that she would do such a thing to me because I was always so genuine with her. However, she always threw shade and did things to hurt me purposely. I remember the boy on our street I had a crush on. Marcell.

He was the cutest boy ever. Just how she swore she couldn't stand Keyon, she was the same way with Marcell. One day, my mother made me go with her to church. For some reason, Mera ditched us this day because she would always tag along. Missing church was like missing school so I was eager to get back home. When we made it to our street, I went to Mera's and she wasn't home. Instead of going home, I stopped by Marcell's. I knocked on the door and got no answer and because his mother's car was gone I assumed his family was at church also.

I don't know why but I walked around to the side door and I could hear music coming from inside the home. Curiosity got the best of me so I went to Marcell's bedroom and peeked inside. Mera was laying on his bed and he was sitting on the side of her with his hands inside her shorts. I would never forget the light moans that escaped her lips as she moved back and forth. When I say my heart was crushed, I was so hurt. I ran home and buried myself in my room and cried myself to sleep.

When I finally brought this to Mera's attention she swore she didn't know I liked him. I found that odd because she was the one always singing "Chas and Cell sitting in a tree, K-I-S-S-I-N-G." Anytime he was around, I would blush so hard it was evident to the world I liked him. And here it was, she didn't know.

"SO YOU DIDN'T HAVE no idea she was fucking that nigga?" He asked bringing me from my thoughts. Finally, I turned around to face him. I was slightly embarrassed because of his question but I was gonna be truthful.

"To be honest, all the signs were there but I ignored them. We were like sisters more than best friends, so I would never imagine her doing such a thing. It's crazy because she swore she couldn't stand him. She was the one always telling me about the rumors of him messing with other girls, and I didn't see then that she was trying to just break us up. It's like she didn't care about hurting me. Me and Keyon had been together since we were young, and Mera was always our third wheel. I guess I was just young, dumb and ignored the signs."

I dropped my head and a few tears slid down my face. "My roommate Nancy kept telling me something wasn't right and because I valued our friendship I brushed it off. The night Keyon and I were gonna..." I stopped talking for a few moments remembering that night I almost gave myself to him and it made me began to cry harder. "I was gonna give him me, ya know?" I began choking up.

The mention of that night made his face ball up. Those cold eyes appeared and like he always did, he got up from the bed and walked into the restroom. I laid there drowning in my tears because everything in my life was a blur at this moment. My best friend had deceived me, my boyfriend who I thought loved me was dead, and I was held against my will behind my father's inconsiderate ways. That same feeling of wishing I was dead when I was younger had resurfaced. Right now, I felt like I didn't have anything to live for so, again, I wished he'd just pull the trigger and get it over with.

T he sound of my ringing phone made me look over towards the dresser. It was 3 AM and normally when my phone rang at this time it wasn't good. Before reaching over, I looked over to Chastity who was in a deep slumber. I chuckled to myself because of the drool that ran from the corner of her mouth dripping down to her pillow. Her face was stained with dried tears from crying herself to sleep. Little mama was beyond hurt because of her friend's disloyalty; and here I was only adding to her already gloomy heart.

"What's up?" I answered my phone seeing that it was Kill.

"What's up Lege. Aye, Columbus hit me and said they found the truck." I sat up straight just hearing those words. "No sign of Roberts or the work though." he sighed into the phone frustrated. "But check it, it's a few messages on ol girl phone. I just need the code." Hearing this piqued my interest wondering if any was her pops. Again, I looked at her and wanted so bad to wake her up. But because this was the best sleep she had gotten since the kidnap I decided to let her sleep.

"I'll get it when she wake up."

"When she wake up? Nigga where y'all at?"

"A room."

"Man, you ain't tryna fuck her is you?"

"Hell naw nigga. Soon as this nigga turn my shit over I'mma let her go."

"And how you know she ain't gone tell?" he asked and he had a point. I had been contemplating that same question and I was having seconds thoughts of letting her go. After the clip on the news today, I was really unsure. They had a missing report out for her and seeing how gullible she was, I just knew she would roll over on a nigga.

"I don't know." I shook my head. I was getting tired of this shit myself. And now hearing they found my truck let me know Allen had moved my shit or sold it.

"You think them Mexican muthafuckas working with Allen?"

"At this point ain't no telling."

"I mean, think about it, who the fuck that nigga know that he could sell 100 birds too? We both know Allen and he ain't shit but a gambleholic on a verge crackhead."

"And that's my fear." I shook my head. "This nigga could have sold the shit for crumbs."

"So what you gone do with her?"

"Nigga, you keep asking me that like I know. Shit, she gone work her pops' debt off."

"Sell some pussy?"

"Shit I don't know. But I'll get up with you in the morning. We gotta meet up with Shaq and cook up some more work. And I need to meet Fedel, drop him off a few."

"Aight. Well, I'll hit you in a couple hours." I looked at the clock and since it was already morning I know I wouldn't be able to sleep. Shit, I couldn't sleep if I wanted to because I didn't trust Chastity.

"Aight one."

"One."

FEW HOURS LATER...

. . .

SITTING at the table with Chastity, I watched her body language as she ate her breakfast. She was looking out the window and she hadn't said a word. I could tell she was feeling some type of way because I asked her for her passcode but owell; I've told her over and over I wasn't sparing her father's life. To my surprise, she gave me the code and since, she's been mute. I still hadn't given it to Kill but since I was meeting him in the next hour I decided to wait.

"Hurry up, Chas, so we can roll." I told her and stood up from the table. The minute I stood up my phone ran and it was Arian. I answered the phone because I figured she wanted something. Arian knew I was a busy nigga so she hardly bothered me.

"Yo?"

"Hey Amad." she said calling me by my middle name. I chuckled a little bit because no matter how many times she heard Legend she refused to call me that.

"Sup Ari."

When I said Ari, Chastity looked over in my direction. Her face was flushed with jealousy and for some reason it made me feel awkward.

"I was wondering if I could borrow one of your cars? My car in the shop until Saturday."

"Aight, I'll swing by to bring it...

"I don't wanna leave. I don't have anything to wear." Chastity spoke on purpose. I looked at her and she wore this *owell* look on her face.

"Who's that?" Arian asked shocking me. She never questioned me about what I did or had going on. Shit, she didn't even wanna be with me.

"That's my little cousin. But aye, I need you to do me a favor."

"Sure."

"I need you to hit the mall and grab me some shit. I need about 10 shirts and 10 pairs of pants." I looked at Chas to size her up. "Size 5 and small in shirts. Also grab some under clothes, bras and underwear, and shit too. Bout a small in panties and 32 C in bra." Chastity looked stunned which confirmed I hit her sizes on the money.

"Wait, you got me shopping for one of your bitches? For real Amad?" she hissed ready to blow.

"Man, I just told you this was my cousin." Chastity rolled her eyes and got up from the table. She headed into the restroom, and I could hear the water running. "Grab some shoes too." I got up and looked at the shoes I had got from the dungeon. Because her feet hung off a little I figured she wore a size 6. "Size 6 and take this out the bread I got at your crib."

"Okay. Well I need the car."

"Aight, give me a minute. I'll be there."

"Okay." she hung up just as Chas walked back into the room. I lifted off the bed and grabbed my keys along with the room key. Because they had basically plastered her face all over the news I decided to just check out. I was gonna just purchase her a bed for the Black Hole. I couldn't risk coming in and out of a hotel just in case someone recognized her. I stood by the door waiting for her to slide her shoes on. She was taking her time on purpose, and it took everything in me not to curse her out. As she walked past me, I slightly pushed her making her stumble a little. She turned around annoyed and caught me chuckling. After closing the door, we headed down the hall. Instead of the elevator, we headed down the stairs so we could bypass the many cameras.

WHEN WE GOT to my whip, I looked around to make sure nothing was out the ordinary. I hit the unlock on my alarm and told Chas ass to hurry and hop in. Climbing into my driver seat, I pressed play on my touch screen and turned up my beat.

LOOK, *no I can't promise commitment, but I swear we'll have fun*
If you ask I'll be honest, girl you not the only one
Just a man on the mission, with my hand on my gun
Couple niggas that hate me, but way more people show love

. . .

Nipsey's *If You Were Mine* played through the speakers and the base pounded so hard it rumbled the rearview mirror. This was my shit so anytime it came on I had it to the max. Chastity laid her head back on the seat as she took in the words. From time to time, I looked over at her and my thoughts were perplexed. Shit was seeming weird as fuck with her being around. The little jealous stunt she pulled had a nigga baffled as fuck. Shit was cute but I didn't understand why.

I looked over her appearance and even in the old raggedy sweats and top she wore she was looking good as fuck. She had took her ponytail down and wet her hair at the room so it was now curly hanging down her shoulders. *Little mama got cute to die.* I shook my head and chuckled to myself. After I got a kick out my thoughts I had to come to terms with myself that this girl wasn't dying any time soon. I don't know why but I didn't have it in me to kill her. I just hoped like hell this shit ain't backfire on me.

"You know how to drive?" I asked Chas as we were nearing our exit. She looked at me confused like the question I asked was a trick question.

"Yeah."

"Aight. I need you to drive this whip. Chas, don't try no bullshit." She didn't respond but she slightly nodded her head. We pulled into the warehouse where I stored my cars and Kill cooked up our work. From in my seat I started the ignition to my AMG and told Chas to follow me. She looked a bit nervous and the shit made me nervous. *Man, I hope this girl can drive.* I shook my head as she got out the whip. Listening for the running motor she walked over and hopped in. I backed up so she could back up and pulled to the side of the road. I grabbed my strap and sat it in my lap then pulled off slowly from the curb.

As I drove towards Arian's crib I knew I couldn't take Chas to her home so I told her to catch an Uber up the street to the McDonalds.

We were only a few miles away so I was gonna slow down to give her some time. Hanging up the phone, I looked into my rearview and noticed Chas was right behind me. Pulling up to a red light, I pressed on the brake to stop and something caught my attention out the corner of my eye. The AMG flew past me running right through the red light. Just in time, the light turned green so I took off in full speed behind it. This chick was tryna get away from me and the shit had me 38 hot.

Doing damn near 100 MPH every time I pulled up on the side of her she sped up. She began weaving through traffic nearly wrecking at least 3 times. She made a sudden left turn so I banked the corner with her. I sped up and got on the side of her. I rolled my window down and grabbed my strap. I sent 5 bullets into the car and through the window. I could hear her screams. She was so caught up in me busting at her she quickly hit the brakes making the car jerk. I jumped out my whip and snatched her dumb ass out the car. I put her in my other car and pointed my gun at her head.

"1,2,3,4,5,...." I began counting to calm my nerves.

"I'm sorry." she was crying hysterically but that shit fell on deaf ears. I pulled out my phone and dialed Arian. I instructed her to stay in the Uber and just come get the car. After giving her the location to the car I got out to stash the key inside. When I climbed back into my whip I looked over at Chas who was still balling her eyes out.

"You can wipe them dumb ass tears off yo face shorty. I swear it's taking everything in me not to kill yo ass. You dumb as fuck yo." I shook my head as I pulled off from the curb.

Her dumb ass was going back to the dungeon and because of this move she pulled I wasn't buying her dumb ass no bed. Just when I was trying to be lenient with her she had to fuck it up. I swear right now she was lucky because my trigger finger was itching.

10

CHASTITY

I sat in his passenger seat, legs shaking, hands shaking and even my lip quivered as tears ran down my face. I was so scared; if he didn't kill me then, he would for sure kill my ass this time. I couldn't believe he shot at me; scratch that, I could believe it because he was crazy as hell. The look in his eyes told me he wanted to kill me now but I didn't understand why he didn't. Instead he shot at the back of the car and one bullet pierced through the driver door missing my leg by an inch.

From time to time I stole glances in his direction. I knew he was upset because the scowl on his face and the way his jaw was clenched. Normally, he'd have this sense of peace on his face but not today. He was driving fast as hell and hadn't even made me put on the blindfold.

AFTER AN HOUR we pulled up to the familiar parking lot; the dungeon. He jumped out the car and ran over to my side. Forcefully snatching the door open, he yanked me out and pulled me into the building. He walked me past his staff who, like always, ignored the fact that this man had a hostage and led me to the door. I wanted so bad to scream but I was too afraid. With the power he had over these people, it wouldn't do any justice.

As I crossed the threshold that led to the dungeon room, I locked eyes with the same Hispanic woman who seemed to be the only person worried. She held this sincere and sympathetic look in her eyes and the way our eyes connected I was sure she understood my cry for help.

Again I was led into my *now* jail cell and *he* shoved me inside. *Great Job Chastity.* I thought looking around the room then to the bullshit cot of a bed. I laid down on it and turned to my side. My eyes fell onto the door that was in the room and for the first time I got up and walked over to it. Using the tip of my fingernails I tried to see if it would at least budge but it didn't. After trying for a few moments I realized I was wasting my time so I went back to lay down.

A fresh set of tears began to pour from my eyes uncontrollably. I was tired of this shit. I was tired of being here so I needed to think of something and quick. *Maybe if I be nice I could reel him in.* I thought as turned to lay on my back. Tears fell from the corner of my eyes as I stared out the small window. It was still sunny outside and this only hurt more. I thought of those Sundays back on campus when Mera would come to my dorm and basically drag me outside. We would dress in our sunny wear and go watch Keyon an Jason's football practice.

Afterwards we would all go to either a campus party or out to eat. Even with the disloyalty of Mera and Keyon, I would trade it any day for the situation I was in now. I had a future ahead of me. I only had a year left to graduate and because of all the time I was missing I would have to make it up. Even if I made it out of here, things wouldn't be the same. Not only would I have to bust my ass twice as hard but my friendship with Mera was for sure over, Keyon was dead and the thought of this man killing my father would ruin the rest of my life. *Sigh.*

～

Legend
    2 days later...

"OH GOD, what have I done. Chastity baby, it's daddy. I'm so sorry, I'm sorry. Baby please tell me you're okay. If you get this message I..I..I don't have a number for you to call right now but I swear I'll fix this. I just need time to fix this."

KILL and I listened to the last of 3 messages that Allen had left on Chastity's phone. The sound of my phone ringing interrupted us.

"HELLO?"

"Lege, I need you guys to get out of there now!" hearing the rattled sound of Columbus voice made me look over to Kill. Without responding I disconnected the call.

"We gotta move! Kill, pull the truck out with the work on it and I'mma get ol girl. Meet me at my crib."

"Man, I know you not taking her to your crib. What if they come there?"

"I got that under control don't trip. I ain't got a choice. I can't risk someone seeing her out in public. Right now we ain't got time. I gotta get her out." I grabbed the walkie talkie from the desk drawer and headed for the black hole so I could snatch Chas up. There was no telling what this nigga Allen would tell them muthafuckas. Because he had been with the company so long he knew too much. I really wasn't worried bout the work because Kill was gonna pull the truck out and the work in the warehouse was stashed inside of the animals. I also knew that they had to have a proper search warrant. If they were here to get Chas then they could only look for her. Even if they stumbled up on my work it would be ruled out as illegal search and seizure.

. . .

UNLOCKING THE DOOR, I stepped inside and walked over to Chas.

"Get up now; we gotta go." she looked up with that same attitude but right now wasn't the time. "Get the fuck up now!" I yelled making her jump. Hearing the authority in my voice she quickly got up.

"Code red sir... their swarming us." my worker Carlos spoke into the walkie talkie.

"10-4." I replied and pulled Chas towards my emergency exit. I hit the small rusted color button that blended with the wall and when the door popped open Chas' eyes lit up wide as saucers. I knew what she was thinking. This shit had been here all along. But no matter if she searched this entire place she would have never found it. I was willing to bet even if she had to search for it again she still wouldn't find it.

PULLING Chas down the long tunnel I tried hard to swat the spider webs with my free hand. When she wrapped her hand into mines I knew she was nervous and even though I was still mad at her ass the feeling of her hand squeezing mines let me know she trusted me. The tunnel was pitch black and hadn't been used in years which is why it had accumulated so many spider webs and dust.

"What's going on?" she whined out. I ignored her because what could I really say? Your punk ass pops sent the police to my shit. After the stunt she pulled the other day I didn't trust her so I kept quiet.

WHEN WE MADE it to the end, I changed the frequency to channel 13 "10-20 tunnel." I spoke into the walkie talkie and waited for Julio to reply.

"Diez - noventa nueve." he replied in Spanish letting me know I was secure to exit. I pushed the door open and was met with the sun. I pulled Chas arm harder and led her to the unmarked car that awaited us with California Exempt plates that I had got from Columbus. I made her climb into the back while I got into the front. I threw on the cowboy hat and shades once again complementary of Columbus.

As we made our way out into the traffic, I peered down the street where my warehouse was. I could see a swarm of police cars lined out front. The tunnel my father had built led to an opening in my lot but with money and a trusted friendship I expanded it to a nearby warehouse. In the warehouse they had all types of shit going on from housing immigrants, to cooking crystal meth. I gave them my word to use their warehouse as an escape and in return I allowed them to use mines. Because it was my idea I paid to finish building it and thanks to the many immigrants, I paid prolly half the cost I would have paid construction workers.

As CHAS and I drove towards my crib, I was finally able to relax. *That was a close call.* I thought letting out a breath I had been holding for a minute. From time to time I looked over at Chas and she too looked more relaxed. Although she didn't know what was going on, I'm sure she had a clue because of the many police cars that were nearby. I thought about the message from her pops and I envisioned his ass crying. That nigga knew he had put his daughter in a fucked up predicament and this is exactly the reaction I needed. Thinking back on the call, it was something about the sound in the background that caught my attention. The sound was too familiar but I couldn't put my finger on it. When I made it home I was gonna play the recording again and again until I cracked it.

11

LEGEND

When Chas and I pulled up to my crib, I climbed out the car and informed her to get out. I turned around to watch her and in the same time I watched the security gates shut behind us. Turning around, I put in the code to shut off my alarm. We walked into my crib and Chas looked around amazed. My crib was big as fuck but also lonely. Nobody occupied it but me and the maid I had that I had pulled from the Slaughter *Lumida*.

Lumida was one of my pops' favorite workers. She had been around for years just as Allen so I took a liking to her. She was now much older and I could see the hard labor at the Slaughter was weighing heavy on her so I pulled her from the company to come work for me at my crib. She spent most of her time in her room sewing. I didn't mind because she made sure to do what she was supposed to do around my crib. She was a nice lady and every lady at the company wished they had it like her. I don't know but it was something about her I fell in love with.

Lumida was Hispanic like most of my workers but she was abandoned by her family at 14 years old. Her pops had tried to rape her and her mom didn't give two fucks so she ran away. Lumida had told me this story a million times and each time I listened like it was the first. No lie, the shit made me upset especially because what my mom went through.

"Is this your mother?" Chastity's voice made me look over. She looked back over to the picture and studied it for a short moment.

DING!

SAVED BY THE BELL, I thought walking towards my door. I really didn't feel like having the conversation with Chas about my mother. I was still mad at her so I was gonna be stubborn just like her. I walked to the door knowing it was Kill. When I opened the door he wasn't alone. Columbus had joined him and this was perfect because I needed to holla at him.

"Lumida!" I called out to her and waited for her to enter. When she walked in I instructed her to take Chas to the back and get cleaned up. I also told her look through the old room where I kept some of the new shit I had copped Arian. The shit was old but no matter how old it got it was designer shit that cost a grip. "Lumida." I called out to her again. "No telefono." I informed her and she nodded her head. I was sure she read the look in my eyes because that's how we connected.

WE ALL HEADED to my den and took a seat.

"Kill, you handle that?" I asked in reference to the truck.

"It's at the safe." I nodded my head and looked at Columbus.

"What this shit was about today Lumbus?"

"Well, I'm not sure if Allen called in because the voice was from a woman. However, he could have put someone up to it. The raid wasn't for a kidnap; it was for ICE the Immigration and Customs Enforcement. So they were basically coming to deport and search for illegal immigrants. Now, if it were Allen he didn't want to mention his daughter being held captive which is odd. I'm sure it was because of the drugs he stole and he didn't want to have to explain that. You don't have to worry about anything because everyone has their citizenship." he stated but more of a question. I nodded my head *yes* because I made sure to have everyone's green cards. Most of the staff were citizens and the others I spent a pretty penny on. One thing about the Slaughter, I made sure my shit was intact. I had too much illegal shit going on not to.

"Here the 911 call." Columbus said and pushed play on a hand device. Just as the voice spoke, Kill and I looked at one another. On cue "Liliana." we said it at the same time. Liliana was one of the workers at the Slaughter. For some reason I had a funny feeling about her because ever since Chas had been there she had been giving me these odd looks.

"Handle her Kill." I told Kill and he already knew what time it was.

"So they should be leaving soon?" Kill asked looking at Columbus.

"After checking everyone's information they should be gone. I'll get the call." Columbus stood to his feet to make his exit. I nodded my head and Kill stood up to let him out. When he walked back over, he took his seat. Remembering the voice message I pulled out Chas phone and began to listen.

"Nigga listen to this. Tell me what it sound like?" I leaned over to put the phone up so we both could hear clearly. Allen began to whine into the phone and we bypassed his voice and focused on the sound in the background.

"Manayunk church bell." Kill looked at me certain. I jumped to my feet hyped. I knew I knew the sound from somewhere. I just couldn't put my finger on it.

"This nigga in Philly." I told Kill shaking my head. "Hit that nigga Columbus. Let him know, find any nigga that move any work in Philly and holla at any muthafucka that run a gamble shack or anything associated."

"I'm on it." Kill stood up and was preparing to make his exit.

Although I gave the orders and demands, I wanted this nigga Allen to myself. If I had to go to Philly personally, his blood was mine. I wanted this nigga and I wanted him bad. It wasn't even bout the money; like I said before, it was the muthafuckan principle. I fed this nigga and I fed him good. And if it was one rule I learned in these streets, it was never bite the hand that feeds you. Period. I let out a deep sigh because this was the beginning of my mission. It was gonna be a long week and I could feel it.

I WAS LAYING BACK on my sofa and it's like I could smell her aroma a mile away. I knew she was coming down the hall so I focused on the television. When she came into view, I could see she was looking for me out the corner of my eye. When she found me, she walked over and stood at the opposite side where my feet rested.

"Ummm...I'm kinda hungry. I was gonna ask Lumida but I didn't wanna wake her." she spoke uncertain with a hint of fear. My eyes fell onto the shorts and top she was wearing and I sized her up. The light from the television danced off her skin and even in the shadows I could still see her innocent eyes. As bad as I wanted to tell her to starve, I got up and made my way towards the kitchen with her close behind. She took a seat at the island and I began looking in the fridge for whatever Kemp had whipped up. He was the chef that came to cook twice a week. And even though I was hardly home I didn't mind because Lumida loved his cooking.

Finding a plate with the cover on it, I pulled it out and took the lid off. Chastity's eyes darted over to the metal tray and hunger filled her eyes. I chuckled to myself as I slid the tray of parmesan chicken, garlic butter mashed potatoes, string beans and rolls into the oven. I looked over at Chas to tell her the food would be ready shortly and I noticed her eyes fixated on the mail that sat on the counter top. *Damn* I thought because I was slipping.

"Man yo ass nosey." I snatched up the mail and mugged her.

"Well it's good to finally have a name to put with the face of the man that's held me captive for nearly two weeks. You know I was getting tired of calling you him, that man or asshole. She smirked with her little smart ass.

"You could have been asked."

She rolled her eyes and I could tell I pissed her off.

"Anyway, Legend, you might wanna read that. It's from the Department of Child Support Services." her cocky ass said rolling her neck.

"I don't know why, I ain't got no seeds." I shot then picked up the envelope. I tore it open but I made sure not to take my eyes off her. Finally focusing in on the letter I began reading.

Dear Legend Gambino,

We have been informed that there is a possibility that you could possibly be the father of [Makalah Cummings] Case No: 362001. We have scheduled for a mandatory appointment for a DNA test to be taking place on....

I stopped at father of, because there was no way in hell. I strapped up with every bitch I stuck my dick in, including Arian. This shit had to be some type of hoax. I read the paper over and over then looked at the envelope to make sure the shit was properly sealed. Sure enough it had a government stamp on the front. I was so into my thought that I didn't even notice Chas grab her food and walk past me. Before she got to the table to sit and eat she looked back and smirked.

"Rolling stone." she shot over her shoulder then walked off to the dinner table.

This girl was gonna be an annoying pain in my ass and it was evident after today. I wanted to run behind her and choke her ass out because this shit was serious. I had a bitch trying to plant a baby on me that wasn't even mines. I knew for a fact the child wasn't mines but still, whoever this bitch was, was playing games and wasting my fucking time. I was gonna show up to the testing so whoever it was could get off my back. Fuck proving a point because I ain't have to prove shit to whoever this bitch was nor the punk ass court system. I looked over the paper again and realized the test date was tomorrow. There's no telling how long this letter had been sitting here because I never checked the mail. In fact, Lumida checked it and there was never anything important.

WALKING BACK into the living room I took a seat back on the sofa. I grabbed the remote and began flicking through channels. After about thirty minutes Chas came in and made herself comfortable. I looked in her direction because nobody told her ass to sit down. She looked at me, watching her and she dropped her head. Like always she began twirling her thumbs and I knew then she had something to say.

"So was it my father that called the cops?" she asked without looking at me.

"I don't know who it was." I kept it short then turned back to the TV.

"So what's gonna happen? What happens if he never appears?"

"Oh he's gonna appear." I snarled thinking of him being in Philly. I turned the TV up to drown out Chastity's voice. I was hoping she got the hint and shut the fuck up. Shit was already confusing and it didn't help that I couldn't give her a straight up answer. It's like she wanted me to say "I'm gonna kill you." but how could I?

WHEN THE WORDS rape crossed the screen I focused in on the Caucasian newscaster.

Hi, I'm Kimberly Walters reporting live from Kensington Avenue where a woman, Black, ages 22-28 was raped and murdered. At the moment, we have no information about the victim nor the suspect. We have one witness

that said she heard screaming but was too afraid to go near the dark alley
you see behind me. We're asking anyone if you have any information please
contact 26th District Police Department at (215) 686-3260.

I LOOKED over to Chas because I could hear light sniffles letting me
know she was crying. Indeed, she had tears pouring down her face
and it made me wonder what was going through her mind. I was
fucked up watching it also just thinking bout my moms. The shit was
fucked up and to think I had to visit Philly soon. I was ready to head
out soon as we got some type of word. I had people from Philly and
with the money I had it gave me a little power to be able to connect
with people inside. I had Kill on it and Columbus as well. It's like I
could just feel it in my soul that nigga was there and soon I would
find out.

12

CHASTITY

When Legend looked in my direction I tried hard to wipe away the tears that had fallen from my eyes. Anything that associated with rape was always so touchy to me. It was sad how a man could forcefully take something that belonged to you without your permission. Not to mention take a woman's life for something that was hers. The shit was sickening and hearing that took me back to that place.

From the corner of my eyes Legend watched me so I stood to my feet and left the room. I'm sure he would think I was just some emotional girl but no one would understand unless they were in my and that woman who lost her life shoes.

I headed into the room that Lumida had instructed me to sleep in and took a seat on the bed. I looked around the room and it was nice for it to have been a guest room. I could tell that no one visit often because the smell of new wood from the headboard lingered through the air. I haven't took a tour of the home but I was sure there were more rooms because the home was huge. I laid back and thought of the possibility of escaping when he went to sleep. I knew I was gambling because of the security gate outdoors. It was huge. Too damn huge for me to jump. On the way in I looked around his landscape for any neighbors but I came up short. His land was so spacious you couldn't even see a home nearby except for the homes that were far away on the top of a mountain. Letting out a sigh I thought long and hard until the sound of his voice brought me from my thoughts.

"You straight?" he peeked his head into the room. Ignoring him I just laid there and remained quiet. He walked away and headed in the opposite direction of the living area. I laid in this spot deep in thought and before I knew it, nearly an hour had went by. I climbed out the bed and wandered down the hall in the direction I saw him go. Every door I passed by was shut except the two restrooms I passed by. Already I was on a whole other side of the home and here were a pair of stairs. I stood there and began to bite my bottom lip wondering what could have been up there.

"Chastity." I jumped hearing my name. I held my hand over my chest because Lumida had scared the shit out of me.

"Ju okay Mija?"

"Umm..yeah..I was looking for..ummm."

"Last door." she pointed then turned to walk away. I walked towards the door she pointed out and a lump formed in my throat. The door was slightly ajar so I pushed it open and stepped inside. My mouth hit the floor and not because of the huge beautifully decorated room. Legend stood there naked as the day he was born. When he spent around it looked like he had a third leg that spent with him. I couldn't help it, I watched it in awe because I had never seen anything like it. I thought of the day Keyon and I were about to have sex for the first time and his wasn't nearly the size of Legend's.

"It's called knock." he said and smirked.

"Uhhh..I..I'm sorry." I turned and ran out as fast as I could. I went into the room and buried myself underneath the covers. I couldn't get the size of him out my mind. The middle of my legs began to throb and this was something I've never experienced. It's like I couldn't stop it and the more I thought of him the more it throbbed. Squeezing my legs tightly together wasn't any help. I turned over on my stomach and tried my hardest to doze off. I tossed and turned until, finally....

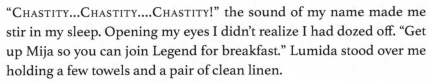

"CHASTITY...CHASTITY....CHASTITY!" the sound of my name made me stir in my sleep. Opening my eyes I didn't realize I had dozed off. "Get up Mija so you can join Legend for breakfast." Lumida stood over me holding a few towels and a pair of clean linen.

"What time is it?"

"It's morning, 7:32." she replied and I could tell she was ready to get to work. She passed me a brand new toothbrush so I climbed out of bed and headed into the restroom. I began washing my face and brushing my teeth then wet my hand so I could brush the wild strands of hair back off my face. I headed out the restroom and down the hall towards the kitchen. When I walked in, Legend was seated at the table stuffing his face. Assuming the plate across from him was mines I took a seat in front of it.

"I gotta make a run today. Lumida is gonna be here if you need anything. I also have one of my guards that's gonna be here to watch yo little slick ass." I didn't bother to reply because there was really nothing to say. I picked up my fork and began eating the scrambled eggs with cheese.

"Anything you need while I'm out?"

"Um..my books."

"Books? I thought you was gonna say some girl shit. Pads, tampons all that other shit girls need."

"I don't wear tampons because they hurt but yes I do need pads, Dove soap and Oxy face wash for sensitive skin. I don't know if there's a brush in there but I need one. And yes I said books. I have one year left of school, Legend, so I don't wanna miss out. It will be like I went all these years for nothing." he looked at me but didn't say a word. Like always, there was a faint pause. Finally he nodded his head okay and I couldn't believe he agreed.

"Write them down. I'm not going all the way to your school but I can get any book you need." he lifted up and headed into the kitchen. He came back shortly after carrying a pen and piece of paper. I jotted down all the books I needed which was a total of nine books.

"Damn why so many books. Fuck you studying in?"

"Law. I'm on my Juris Doctor Degree then I have to take my Bar exam. I graduated high school early so I did my pre-reqs at a community college. Then I received a scholarship to go to Duke." he nodded his head impressed.

"That's what's up...well I'm bout to head out. Don't do no dumb shit. And FYI ain't no phones around here and trust me you'll never be able to hop that gate."

I rolled my eyes as he stood to leave. I watched him grab his keys and head towards the door. Before he exited, he lifted his shirt to show me his gun and winked. Again, I rolled my eyes and turned around.

As I BEGAN PICKING through my eggs I was so caught up in what Legend said I couldn't even eat. Lumida walked into the room and headed into the kitchen. I could see her out the side of my eye staring at me from behind the counter.

"Don't look like that Mija. He's not bad as you think. Senor is a great guy once you get to know him. And I tell he really likes you."

"Lumida, I don't know if you know why I'm here and it's not my place to speak on because your loyalty is with Legend. But, anywho, he don't like me. He treats me so mean." I dropped my head and forked at my eggs.

"No fight the feeling. Whatever happens let it happens. But trust me, if he was gonna kill ju, will been muerta." she sassed and turned to walk away. Exactly what she said I've thought of. Just like when I tried to escape, he could have killed me but he didn't. However, I was still a damn prisoner. Legend didn't want me and I didn't want his ass. To be real, he was too much for me especially after what I saw last night. That man was handcrafted by God and he took his time making his private parts. Like Beyonce said, he got a big ego and a big dick to go with it.

· · ·

I CLOSED my eyes just thinking about the sight of him. Just like last night my middle part began to throb between my legs. I was gonna forever have that vision of him etched in my mind. I opened my eyes to the sound of the door slamming. Thinking it was Legend I turned around but was met with a man that stood at least seven feet. He looked at me and I could see the seriousness in his face. His nose frowned, but his eyes got to me. They were a light brown like mines but creepy. I figured this was the person that was gonna look over me. Just his presence alone annoyed me so I got up from the table and headed into the kitchen to wash my plate.

"Lumida got it. Head on to the room." he said in a heavy voice that traveled through the home. I let out a sigh in frustration and slammed the plate into the sink. I walked towards the room and as I was just nearing the hall door he shot some slick shit to me. Not giving him my energy I headed into the room and laid down on the bed. Lumida had laid out some clothing for me so after the nap I was gonna take, I was gonna take a shower. I couldn't believe I was gonna say this but, I hoped Legend was back soon. I did not like the fact that he had this creep ass man guarding me.

13

LEGEND

"**Y**ou staying for dinner?" Arian asked as she pulled out her chinaware to begin setting her dinner table. As bad as I wanted to stay to eat her fire ass cooking I needed to get home. It's been two days since I left Chastity because I needed to relieve some built up nut that was clogged in my sack. Yesterday, I spent time with both Stacy and Megan and today Arian got me over by using my car as an excuse. No lie, I been missing her ass but I was too occupied with this whole shit with Allen. Not only that but Chastity. Since I've been here I've been thinking of her little ass. It's like she gave me a sense of peace with no effort. In my mind I told myself sooner or later I would have to kill her because like Kill said she would for sure tell, however, my heart clouded what may have been my better judgment.

After the horrific shit I dealt with with little man I had killed years ago, I couldn't bring myself to kill her. Although I didn't give a fuck about Allen, Chas didn't deserve to die. She was a good girl with a pure heart and everyday it showed. The other day when she asked me to bring her books that shit touched the little soft spot I did have. Out of all the things she could have asked for she asked for books. And guess what? I got her books. I had to pay a pretty penny for them but it didn't matter. I hoped like hell her ass could do an online course because I couldn't let her go unless I would be able to sit in class with her. Keep shit real I was willing to. Her asking me for her books let me know how important her education was to her. The way her eyes lit up when she mentioned her major she was electrified. She was young with goals and that shit was sexy as hell.

"Nah ma, I gotta roll. My cousin at the house." I lied without looking at Arian. I couldn't even look her in the face because she would see right through me. This girl knew me like a book and deep down she knew there was no fucking cousin. Arian knew my entire family and I never mentioned no damn aunties with any daughters.

"Oh okay. Well when you coming to get the car?"

"Just bring it to the crib like tomorrow or something."

"Okay." she replied and I could hear the disappointment in her voice. I walked over to her and placed a kiss on her cheek. I watched her as she put two plates down on the table and I frowned.

"I'm not staying so why you putting two plates down?"

"Because I might have company."

"Yeah aight." I chuckled because she was trying to get under my skin. I walked towards the door and didn't say shit else. Just because we weren't in a relationship, so she say, Arian knew not to play with me. I walked to my whip and keep shit real, I wanted to duck off outside to see who she thought she was gonna have over. I swear on my mama I would air this entire block out if she thought she was gonna have a nigga in her crib. Just the thought alone made me wanna say *yeah I'mma stay* but Chastity departed me from her.

CLIMBING into my whip the music came on and I bust my U turn to head home.

WE STARTED *off as close friends (Close friends)*
   Somehow you turned into my girlfriend (My girlfriend)
   We used to tell each other everything (Everything)

I even went and bought her diamond rings, matching earrings

I DIDN'T CARE for the mumble rap music but this nigga Lil Baby was hard. I bopped my head to the song as I floated on the highway home. I was like Omarion speeding to get to Chas. Don't get it fucked up, I was still mad her but I couldn't wait to see her fake ass smirk she hid behind her smile.

WHEN I PULLED up to my crib, I grabbed Chas books, hopped out and damn near ran inside. I opened the door to my crib and it was dark as fuck. Normally, Lumida had the kitchen light on and a white candle lit in the den. She always lit candles for peace and for so long I laughed until I understood, protect your peace. When I came home I was always peaceful. A nigga dealt with so much in the streets I needed this shit at home to calm me. I lived a crazy ass life. One would think I ran a normal company cutting cows and pigs but that wasn't the case. My drugs were what was important to me and as long as them birds reached their buyer I was satisfied. I didn't push 2, 3, birds at a time. Each sale was twenty and more a brick and anything less I wasn't wasting my time.

As I WALKED down my long ass hallway, I thought of the look on Chas face when I gave her the books. I knew she would be happy even though she tried to play tough. Nearing her room, I stopped in my tracks because the sound of unpleasant cries could be heard seeping under her door. It sounded like pleading until I heard Chastity's voice cry out "Noooo." I pulled my strap from my waistband and eased down the hall like a thief in the night. When I got to Chas room I pushed the door open and I couldn't see shit but Ron's huge frame bent over the bed. I walked further into the room and nearly lost it. He had just pulled his pants down and Chas was fighting him off of her screaming at the top of her lungs. That same rush that always formed in my body uncontrollably came rushing through. Right now I didn't have time to count. Shit my mind wouldn't let me count. I pulled my strap out and pumped three bullets into his body. He turned around like he didn't understand what was happening but when he saw my face his face frowned in confusion. However, he couldn't grasp on what was happening because blood began to seep from his mouth. He titled his head to the side again not under-standing why he had basically met his maker. With no remorse, I sent another bullet into his head and his body dropped. The sound of Chas' cries made me look over. My chest was heaving and my blood was pumping and seeing her in such a state made me more angered.

"Legend!" she screamed my name but it was like she was happy I came but frightened. She jumped up and ran over to me and fell into my chest. She cried so hard my emotions began to take over. I wrapped my arms around her to let her know she was now safe. Suddenly she pulled back and began screaming shit I couldn't understand.

"I'm tii...I'm tir....You let me...!! Legendddd..oh my god..I'm tired of this shit! I'm tired. Just kill me please! Please just kill me!"

Hearing her say this did something to my soul. I pulled her into me to comfort her. I wanted her to understand she was safe. She was secure now. She tried to fight me but I lightly restrained her.

"Chas, you okay ma. I got you. I got you." I rubbed her back as I looked down at Ron's lifeless body. I couldn't believe this nigga. Ron had been around for years and even though I've never put him in this situation I would never expect him to try and take some pussy.

"Ohh nooo." I heard another voice. I looked towards the door and Lumida wore a frantic look. "Chastity." she called out to her and ran over to us. She pulled her from my embrace as her eyes wandered over Ron's body. "Let's go Mija." she pulled her out the room. Lumida knew already what time it was. She was very familiar with *The Corner* but never have I had to call them to my home. Like I said before this was our peace; they prolly didn't even know where I stayed. I pulled out my phone and sent a text. I knew they would be here in no time. I walked out and left Ron's body laid out. I walked up the hall towards

Lumida's room and opened the door. Lumida was now in her room on both knees praying to the statue she kept on her nightstand. When I didn't see Chas I closed the door and headed to my room which was the last door next to Lumida's.

When I pushed the door open she was sitting on my bed crying so hard I was sure her tears had fallen onto my plush carpet. I ran over to her side and dropped to my knees. As bad as I wanted to go back into the room and send more shots into Ron's body Chas needed me.

"I just wanna die. I'm tired of going through this." she cried as my hands rested on her knees. I was certain what she meant because the last incident when Jose had violated her and now this.

"I'll never leave your side again. I promise. Not even for five minutes Chas." she was still talking reckless as tears poured down her angelic face. "I swear I'll never leave your side again. I grabbed her hands so she would know I was serious. I lifted up from my knees and laid her back on my bed. She was still crying but this time she didn't try to fight me. I pulled the cover over her because she was wearing only a t-shirt and a pair of panties. I peeled out my clothes and climbed in the bed with her. I instantly pulled her into my arms and she rested her head on my chest. After laying there for a few moments her breathing subsided and that told me she felt safe with me.

I let out a deep sigh feeling like shit. I was already causing her enough grief and now for the second time while in my care she was dealing with some crazy shit. Although she may not have understood how I felt about a rapist, pedophile, and anything in that nature, I needed her to understand I would kill for her. This was the second body I caught over her. Ron been my boy for years and one of my most trusted guards. Shit a lot of people didn't know where I stayed but Ron did. However, for Chas, I would kill again. I trusted Ron and Jose to do me a fav but they deceived me which costed them their lives. Not only that, Chas was special and as bad as I was in denial, I had to come to terms that baby girl meant more to me than expected.

14

CHASTITY

I cried so long and hard that my body had basically shut down and I finally dozed off. When I opened my eyes, my head was spinning like I was in a twilight. The rapid heartbeat from Legend's chest let me know he was still awake but I was too nervous to look up. For some reason I felt secure in his arms as crazy as it may have sounded. This was the second time that I was nearly raped in his care but both times he had murdered men that I was sure he'd known for years. The thoughts of him only letting me survive because of my father were now gone. It was something about the look in his eyes when he pulled that trigger that made me feel secure.

Letting out a deep sigh alerted him that I was now awake and again he began to run his fingers through my hair. Swallowing the lump in my throat I peered up at him and our eyes met. He wore a look of concern and I could tell he was flustered. Breaking our eye contact I laid my head back on his chest. For the first time in a long time he brought me this sense of peace which was confusing. I was supposed to hate this man but I couldn't. Right now he was like my knight in shining armor just like the night my father had finally murdered my attacker.

"I apologize for the shit both them niggas did but I can't take it back. Like I told you, I won't leave your side and as long as you with me I'ma protect you. I know all this shit is confusing. Shit, it's confusing me. I'm supposed to kill you Chas but for some reason I can't bring myself to doing it. Go back to sleep and get you some rest." he said and slid down to get comfortable. Not knowing what to say, I remained quiet and turned to my side. I couldn't stand to face him right now.

When his body slid closer to mines my body tensed up as he wrapped his arms around me. It felt good as hell laying in his arms and just like he said this shit was confusing. I wasn't supposed to feel safe with him but I couldn't help it. The room fell silent so I closed my eyes and tried hard to go back to sleep. Right on cue, he began rubbing my head again and in an instant I could feel my eyes getting heavy. I said a quick prayer to myself and finally shut my eyes. *Sigh.*

WHEN I OPENED MY EYES, Legend wasn't laying next to me but I was still in his bed. The ray from the sun beamed through the window so I knew it was later in the morning. Getting out of the bed I headed down the hall so I could grab my toothbrush and begin my morning hygiene. When I got to the door, I stood froze thinking of the man's lifeless body on the floor. I opened the door and let out a soft sigh when I noticed his body was gone. The pool of blood he once laid in was cleaned up and if I didn't know any better I would have never thought a man was laid out dead just the night before. I quickly ran into the restroom and handled my business. Because I was still in my panties I slid into the shorts that I had on last night and left the room.

Walking down the hall, I don't know why but I had butterflies. When I walked into the living area Legend was seated at the table.

"Y'all gone have to just slide out there without me. But let me hit you back." he spoke into the phone and ended his call. There was a plate in front of him and one across the table like last time. My eyes wandered across the table and fell onto something much more intriguing. A smile crept up on my face as I looked at Legend. Like a kid in a candy store I was excited. I ran over to his side and I hugged him.

"Thaaank you." I said excited.

"You're welcome ma. After we eat you can head upstairs so you can study."

"Okay." I smiled and took a seat.

"So how you feeling?" he asked as he placed the napkin into his lap.

"I'm okay I guess. Thank you for asking."

"Shit it's my duty. A nigga gotta..." he went to say before the door-bell rang. He looked at me for a brief moment then stood to his feet. He walked over to the door but he was now out my view. Moments later he walked back in and the sound of a female's voice could be heard.

"Damn, it smells good in here." she didn't notice me sitting here because she had went straight into the kitchen. The way Legend's house was set up I could see her over by the stove. When she turned around her eyes finally landed on me and she instantly looked at Legend.

"You must be Legend's cousin." she walked over to where I sat and extended her hand. A part of me wanted to say *hell no I'm his prisoner* but instead I nodded my head *yes*. For him to have lied told me this must have been his girlfriend. I don't know why, but an instant jealousy shot through my body so I quickly turned my head. I began to eat and made sure not to look in his direction.

As the girl began babbling, I could feel him stealing glances in my direction. She went from talking about his car to a vacation she wanted to take. It's like she was doing this to get under my skin and it was working. I rolled my eyes and stood to my feet. I didn't want to stay behind and hear another word. I grabbed my books and left the room. I headed down the hall and up the stairs. I don't know where I was going but since he insisted I go upstairs I was gonna find my way.

PUSHING OPEN THE LAST DOOR, I figured this was the room he wanted me in. There was a computer desk with a Mac computer on top, a lounge chair, and a sofa. Along the walls were hundreds of books stacked neatly on the shelves. I walked over to the shelf and began browsing. He had all sorts of Donald Goines books, Kwan, Tranay Adams, The Cartel series but what got me was a book called The Purpose Driven by Rick Warren. It was a novel to help you under-stand the meaning of life. I read the book when I was fifteen years old and I wondered if it was just here for show or did he actually read it.

TAKING A SEAT ON THE SOFA, I dropped my books onto the wooden floor and pulled the throw over my legs. The last thing I remembered my professor going over was End of its Rope and How Killing the Death Penalty Can Revive Criminal Justice. I tried hard to remember the rest but my mind was clouded with thoughts of Legend down-stairs. I wanted so bad to head back down there just to be nosey but I didn't want to impose on him. Cracking open my book, I began to dive in. I had a lot of catching up to do so I was gonna get to it.

THE SOUND of the door opening made me look over. I quickly turned my head when I seen that it was Legend. He asked me was I good but I ignored him. He came further into the room and stood directly in front of me. It took everything in me not to look up at him and he was making it hard for me to concentrate.

"What you working on?"

"Law." I replied short in my most annoyed voice.

"I know that." he chuckled and reached over to lift the book. "What you know about Conviction Litigation?" my eyes shot up amused.

"Where did you learn that, jail?" I rolled my eyes and looked back down to my book.

"Yep. Beat a murder at 19 pro per with your smart ass." he shot and walked out the room. I guess he could tell I had an attitude and now I had pissed him off. *Welp there goes my studying.* I thought as I closed the book.

I HEADED BACK DOWNSTAIRS and found him now sitting in the den. He was on the sofa with his phone in hand and appeared to be texting. I nervously took a seat beside him but I didn't say a word. I guess I had pissed him off because he was ignoring the hell out of me.

"So is that your girlfriend?" I asked to make small talk and it was killing me to know.

"I ain't got no bitch. But since you must know that's my ex." Because he had replied, I made myself more comfortable. I picked up his pack of red vines and when I stuck one into my mouth he looked at me like I was crazy.

"Dang, I can't have none?" I chuckled. When he smiled I felt a whole lot better. I tucked my feet under the pillow because it was freezing.

"Why is it always so cold in here?"

"Cooties." he smirked and looked at me. *Damn he is fine.* I thought lusting over his handsome smile. Legend was the definition of fine. His smile, his body, and even his eyes when they weren't cold black. Keyon was handsome too but not like Legend. His bad boy persona was definitely intriguing and his cocky attitude drove me crazy. If that made sense.

"So what you saying I got cooties?" I matched his smirk.

"Hell yeah. And if you don't get yo cootie ass feet off me I'mma beat yo ass." I burst out into a fit of laughter as I tucked my feet under him.

"You don't like feet?"

"Hell nah. I fucking hate feet yo."

"Mines pretty, see." I kicked one up in the air and wiggled my toes. He began laughing along with me but he examined them.

"Yeah, yo shit aight."

"Well, they bomber when they done." I smiled but he didn't. The room fell silent and we both got lost in a brief thought.

"So tell me why y'all broke up?" I changed the subject and sparked up another conversation.

"Long story." he spoke with a sigh and rubbed his hand over his deep black waves.

"I got all day." I smiled to lighten the mood. He chuckled and stood to his feet. He walked out the room and came back shortly after holding a blanket. He tossed it over me and took a seat. Taking it upon myself, I laid my head on his lap and patiently waited for his story.

"A long time ago my boy paid me ten grand to lure his girl to a room. He was gonna marry her but he wanted to know if she was the one. Anywho, he paid me to be the guinea pig and my dumb ass ended up fucking her."

"Oh no.." my mouth fell open. He shook his head yes and continued.

"Instead of my homie coming, Arian my ex showed up." again my mouth dropped and this mess was juicy.

"So how did she find out?"

"She said find my iPhone."

"So did your friend ever find out?"

"Yeah, shit I told him. I had to because the shit was eating me up. I gave him back his ten bands and never seen or heard from him again." he looked off towards the television but it was evident he was in thought. Whoever his friend was, I could tell he regret costing them their friendship.

I reached my hand up and rubbed the strands of hair on his chin. I must have took him by surprise because he looked down at me and right into my eyes. *Another awkward silence.* I thought because the only thing could be heard was the sound of Will Smith coaching Ashley on the drums. We held each other's gaze and what I did next shocked the hell out of me. Because my hand was still resting under his chin I tugged at his face and pulled him into mines. He didn't object. Instead, he placed a soft kiss on my lips. I closed my eyes expecting a tongue wrestle, however, he pulled back.

I opened my eyes and he was looking down at me. His eyes were confusing because he held lust with a bit of guilt. My heart began to race as I bit my lip embarrassed. Suddenly, he rubbed his hand through my hair and bent down to place a gentle kiss on my lips. I parted my lips open and he slid his tongue inside. Just as our tongues began to have the wrestling match I anticipated, his phone rang so loud we stopped in mid-stride. He picked it up from the side of him which had sunk into the sofa. He looked at the caller ID and quickly answered. He patted my shoulder for me to lift up. I guess he wanted some privacy. He walked out the room leaving me spinning from what had just took place. I couldn't believe what had happened and I'd be a lie if I said it wasn't exhilarating. This was supposed to be all a part of my plan but my plan had become a reality I wasn't ready for.

15

LEGEND

2 WEEKS LATER...

I sat in my office at my desk with my money counter right in front of me. Kill had dropped off the bread from the runs that the Slaughter made and the trap we had out in Jersey. Once I was done I was gonna count it by hand because I didn't trust shit, not even the counter. So far I had 80 grand so I had another 20 to go. As the money flipped through the machine my mind wandered onto Chas who was downstairs studying. Over the past couple weeks I've been trying my best to avoid her. After the day we kissed shit was awkward between us. Well me at least.

I know she prolly thought that I was leading her on, but that wasn't the case. Everything about this girl was impeccable. So perfect, I would really wife her if we had met in another life. Every day I felt myself liking her more and more and the shit was so disoriented. However, I wasn't the husband type and she deserved more than a nigga like me. Not to mention, I had a job to do and she would only confuse my mission more. I couldn't make her fall in love with me then kill her pops because that would be a heartbreak she couldn't take. And if I gave Chas little ass this dick, her ass was fosho falling in love and this was another reason I stayed my distance. I hadn't left the house but I buried myself in my home office watching cameras to the Slaughter. I had too much work in there so I had to make sure my shit was being handled properly.

"SENIOR, there's a woman at the gate fussing to see you." Lumida stuck her head in the door.

"A woman?" I asked confused because she knew Arian and if it was her she would have let her in.

"Jess. Ghetto lady; she has a child with her." I got up from my desk and walked over to the picture window that gave me a view of my entire yard. Standing behind the gate I could see a woman and child but I couldn't make out who she was. I nodded okay to Lumida and headed out the office and to the front bypassing Chas at the table.

When I walked outside I shook my head because this chick I used to smash named Denise was standing there with a furious scowl on her face. I hadn't seen this chick in almost six years so her being here confused me. Hitting the code on the lock box the gate opened and Denise walked in and snatching the young girl by her arms.

"Fuck you doing here?" my head shot back still puzzled.

"Nigga I brought you your daughter. It's been six years and I'm tired. It's time you step up to the plate."

"My daughter? Man gone with that shit." I shot back as I looked at the child she referred to as mines. "I don't know what type of games you playing but ain't no pappy over here." she slammed the papers she was holding in her free hand towards me making me fumble to catch them. I looked from her to the papers twice before reading them. The more I read I thought this had to be some type of joke. I looked at the case number and I remembered the first three numbers which were 362 and that told me this was the child I had taken the DNA for. I looked down the long list of numbers until my eyes fell on, Positive 99.9%. I looked back to Denise who had her hand on her hip with a *told you so* look then I looked down at the little girl.

"Look I ain't got all day. I gotta go to work. Here's her stuff." she pulled a duffle bag from her shoulder and when I didn't reach for it she dropped it to the ground.

"Oh you must be the new girlfriend." I looked behind me and Chas was standing in the doorway. "You look awfully young to be someone's step mom. Well I hope you guys enjoy." Denise said rolling her neck. Without another word she scurried away and out the gate leaving the child and her belongings behind. I looked down at the paper again and I couldn't believe this shit. I had become a father in one damn day and I had no idea what to do. I shook my head and looked down to the paper so I could get the child's proper name. Makalah, I said to myself and looked down at her. Chas stood there just as flustered as me and right now I didn't know what the fuck would come next.

～

"Nigga so you mean to tell me she just dropped her off? Like fuck you fuck the baby, here's your child." Kill asked looking over at Makalah who was seated in front of the television watching *Frozen*.

"Yep." I shook my head.

"Yo this wild yo." he chuckled but more concerned. Kill had kids so he knew about parenting however, this wasn't his responsibility.

"And she said you wasn't shit and that you my daddy so it's yo turn." Makalah looked from the television. I swear she had the neck rolling honest. That ghetto shit came from Denise with her simple ass.

"Just watch TV Makalah." I told her and Kill bust up laughing. Just by the statement she had just made let me know she was smart as hell and I had to watch what I said around her.

Makalah was a pretty ass little girl and the more I looked at her she looked just like a nigga. I looked at the pictures of me as a child and she had me down from my eyes to my lips. Even though her hair was in a wild state, I could tell she had a nice grade of hair.

"Man we gotta go in the office and holla about this nigga Allen." I told Kill and pulled out my phone. I sent a text to Lumida to tell Chas to come here. About a minute later, Chas walked into the living room and when she seen Kill she began fidgeting.

"He cool ma." I assured her. "Aye can you sit right here with little mama while we head upstairs for a minute?"

"Sure." she replied sweetly and took a seat on the sofa. I nodded my head to Kill and we headed upstairs to my office.

WHEN WE WALKED IN, Kill took a seat on the sofa and of course I sat behind my desk to look at my cameras.

"I hollered at Mr. Kim; he sent me this." he reached over and handed me his phone. It was a video of Allen sitting at a poker table inside the Sugarhouse casino. I watched the video closely and he looked mighty comfortable. My face instantly bald up because this nigga wasn't even worried bout his daughter. That message he left on her machine was fake as fuck and the shit was sickening.

"So the nigga is in Philly." I nodded my head. "Send that nigga Shaq up there with James so they can kidnap the nigga. Tell them to just watch the casino for any sight of him. He fasho gone be back."

"Aight. I'ma hit that nigga now."

"What's up with him? I ain't been hearing much from him lately."

"Trap Boy. He sit in that damn Trap all day."

"Nigga be using the Trap as his escape."

"Brittany be driving that nigga crazy. So I'm sure he gonna wanna go. I'ma put Quan in that bitch while Shaq gone."

"Yeah Quan could hold shit down. Man I wish I could just go my damn self."

"Why you can't? Shit we both can go."

"I can't leave ol girl. She might try to escape." he looked at me and tried to read me. "What nigga?" I asked because he was watching me.

"Yo ass. Nigga you in love with that chick."

"Man, miss me with that shit." I waved him off but he wasn't buying it.

"Lege, we been boys for years. I know you like I know my damn self. The last time you had this look on your face was when you was fucking with Arian heavy."

"That's not the case with us. I just need her here to lure Allen in."

Again he looked at me like he knew I was full of shit.

"You gone just sit here and lie to my face like we ain't boys my nigga?" he sat up so he could have a closer view.

"Aight look, man I can't leave because this nigga Ron tried to rape her."

"The fuck you mean he tried to rape her?"

"Shit, I left to handle the business with Makalah and ended up staying with Stacy."

"And Megan." he added. He knew my program all too well.

"Yeah. Then I went to Arian's and stayed over there. When I got back I'm walking damn my hallway and I hear ol girl crying. I open the door, this nigga tryna take the pussy." I shook my head.

"I know you..."

"Damn right. Laid his ass out and let The Corner come get him. Nigga you know I don't play that rape shit."

"Yeah I know." he replied understanding every detail of what I meant. Like I said before, Kill was the nigga to console me when my moms was murdered so he knew how I felt about this type of shit." I leaned back in my seat and looked over at him. "And to answer yo question yeah I like lil baby. I ain't smash but we did kiss."

"I knew it!" he jumped to his feet laughing. "Nigga, you open open. But tell me this, what the fuck you gone do when we kill her pops because she ain't gone forgive you?"

"That's why I ain't fucking with her. We kissed two weeks ago and I been ignoring her since. Keep shit real, I'm fighting temptation because I'm not ready for a relationship and she gone fall in love with a nigga fasho."

"I feel you Lege but shit the way you been acting since she been around, you been a lot calmer. Maybe she what you need. Now I don't know what's gonna happen if you kill her pops but as far as y'all, she's a good girl. Nigga you ain't getting no younger. It's time and shit little mama downstairs needs a step moms." he chuckled. Everything he was saying sent me into a deep thought. He was right. Not only the part about Makalah but a nigga wasn't getting any younger.

After a split second of a sensual daze about Chas, I quickly snapped out of it and changed the subject. Once again I was running from the truth and I really didn't give a fuck. I didn't want no relationship no matter how she had a nigga feeling. Or at least I was trying to convince myself of this.

16

LEGEND

I walked into the living room and stopped in my tracks. I couldn't help but smile just seeing Chas interact with Makalah. They were sitting on the floor with a bucket of popcorn in front of them. Makalah was under Chas because her little ass was apparently scared. They had the house dark while Halloween H2o played on the huge 70-inch screen. I walked over to them and sat down on the ground next to them. I dipped my hand inside the popcorn and Makalah looked over to me with a frown.

"Daddy, why you touching our popcorn? Chastity said you got cooties." she giggled exposing the two silver teeth she had in the front.

"Snitch." Chas playfully hit Makalah making her giggle harder.

"Oh, I got cooties?" I looked at Chas and she instantly began to blush. I pulled her closer to me while Makalah stood froze watching the part where Michael was chasing Jamie down the hall. She began to back up into me and right when Michael swung his knife, Makalah hid underneath my arm.

"Scary ass." I grabbed my baby to let her know she was secure. Another week had went by since Denise dropped her off. The first day, Makalah was comfortable. Shit, it was me who had to get adjusted to her. Every day since, she was growing on me and she was making me enjoy this parenting shit. Her little ass talked too damn much sometimes but she was smart as hell and made me feel warm inside. I couldn't forget about Chas because she had stepped in to help a lot. She kept her hair done, bathed her every night and got her dressed in the mornings. Yesterday Chas and I had went and checked her in school. Well Chas sat her ass in the car along with Kill. I still didn't fully trust her so I had Kill tag along to look after her. Since it was Friday I decided to let her go Monday. Plus I had to find a way to take her shopping. Chas had ordered her a bunch of shit online but I wanted to take them both shopping and out somewhere. I didn't know where because I had to keep Chas hidden.

"So how do you like the whole parenting thing?" Chas asked in a light voice so Makalah wouldn't hear her although she wasn't paying attention anyway. This little girl was really into Michael Myers and the shit was crazy for a 6 year old. I thought about when I was a child I made my moms watch Halloween with me almost every day. No matter how scared I was, I was obsessed with Michael so watching Makalah so in tune with the movie was tripping me out.

"Keep it real, shit cool. She precious as a muthafucka. I feel bad it's been 6 years and I'm just coming into her life."

"It's not your fault Legend."

"I know. I just feel bad. I'mma make up for it though. That bitch ain't never gotta come back and get her. I got her for the rest of her life. I'mma do everything I can to be the best father to her."

"You already are." Chas smiled then dropped her head. I knew she was prolly thinking bout her pops so I didn't know what to really say next.

"*We,* gone make good parents." I smirked to lighten the mood. She lifted her head and began smiling bashfully. Her pretty ass light brown eyes beamed at the thought of us starting something. I said it and I couldn't take it back now. It was too soon to act on it but soon, very soon.

∼

"PUSH ME TOO LEGEND DANG." Chas screamed out as her feet barely touched the ground on the swing.

"Short ass." I shook my head and stepped from Kalah swing to hers. I gave her one nice shove then pushed her two more times. I walked over and did the same with Kalah and once they both had a swingin rhythm I went to take a seat on the blanket. I needed to answer a few texts that Kill had sent to my phone.

As I BEGAN TO SCROLL, from time to time I looked up at Chas and Makalah. I was happy to see them smiling because I didn't expect them to be so excited about coming to a park. This was the only place I felt safe with taking Chastity without someone recognizing her. There was only a couple people here that wasn't nowhere near us. There was also a huge picnic across the way that had just begun to grow. When we first got here they were just setting up and just that fast it was swarmed with people which meant it was about time to roll.

Looking down at my phone, a certain text caught my attention.

SHAQ: *we got those Jordan 12's you wanted that ain't came out.*

JUST READING the text my eyes bucked. My heart began to race and it's like my blood shot through my body like a 737 Max skyrocket. When I looked towards Chas, I noticed a woman walking in our direction. I stood to my feet and began folding the blanket. I picked up Makalah's bag and threw it over my shoulder.

"I knew that was your car. What you doing here?"

"I came to bring my..."

"Daddy, I don't wanna leave." Kalah ran over to me. Megan looked from her back to me.

"Daddy?" her head snapped and she looked back to Makalah. Before I could answer, Chas walked over and took the blanket from my hands. Megan began to eye her and I was hoping she didn't recognize her from the news.

"So this yo new little family? Where this bitch and her baby come from. All this time you got a whole ass family stashed away?" she began tripping. Chas frowned her face and looked at me. I could tell she wasn't feeling all the bitches that Megan had called her and it showed in her body language.

"Legend can we go." Chas grabbed Makalah's hand.

"Legend?" Megan looked at me. "So this yo little family?" she asked for the second time.

"Yep. My wife and daughter. And?" I stepped up on her. "You ain't my bitch for the millionth time so why the fuck do it matter."

Megan looked from me to Chas to me again.

"So what about me?! Nigga you been fucking me all these years and this how you do me!" She began crying and shit. This bitch was crazy in her muthafucking head. I grabbed Chas arm and pulled Kalah by the hand. We turned to leave Megan there shouting to her damn self. Suddenly, I heard Chas scream out "what the fuck!" I stopped in my tracks and Megan was standing there with her fist balled up. *I know this bitch didn't sucker punch her.* I thought ready to beat the shit out of her. Yeah this bitch for sure lost her mind. Before I could get a hold of her neck, Chas ran up on her and began punching her so hard Kalah cringed with every blow.

"Chas!" I called her name and ran over to pull her off of her. As bad as I wanted to let her finish the bitch off I didn't want Chas out here fighting and shit. Can't front though, lil baby fooled the hell out of me. Had a nigga thinking she was young, square and timid, but hell nah, Chas was a Pitbull in a skirt.

"What the fuck y'all got going on over here?" I looked up and Stacy was walking up on us with a huge crowd behind her. A few niggas ran over to Megan while a few mugged me. I whipped my strap from my cargo shorts ready to pop every nigga that tried to run up. When they saw my gun they threw their hands up and began to back up.

"What happened Buck?" Stacy asked looking from me to Megan.

She was wearing a Johnson Family shirt just as Megan and everyone else so that told me it was their family reunion.

"This his bitch and his baby." Megan replied still trying to catch her breath.

"So what that gotta do with you?" Stacy asked. The look on Megan's face told it all. Without warning, Stacy ran up on her and just like Chas she began punching the shit out of Megan. "Dirty bitch!" Stacy was yelling and this was my cue to leave. I still had my strap pointed on these niggas as I told Chas get Makalah who was being nosey as hell. You would think she would be crying but hell nah her little ass was tryna see what the fuck was going on.

WHEN WE GOT to the car I could tell Chas had an attitude and I couldn't say I didn't blame her. After she buckled Kalah in her booster seat she hopped into the passenger seat and slammed the door. She forcefully put on her seat belt and turned to look out the window. Her little pouty lips looked sexy as hell and I found it cute how she was always jealous. I knew right now she was mad about the fight but because the day Arian had come over and she got jealous I knew that played a part also. Right now I was trying hard to focus on the text I had received from Shaq but I couldn't because of these miserable bitches. I couldn't wait until I got a hold of Megan myself. That ass whooping Chas and Stacy had put on her wasn't enough. The shit was amusing as hell but it wasn't enough.

"I apologize about that shit ma." she ignored me just as I expected. "Chas say something."

"Ain't shit to say so please just leave me alone." she turned from me and looked back out the window. Yeah I was gone leave her ass alone alright. I couldn't wait till we got to my crib cause it was time I put her in her place. She was about to wake a sleeping giant and I wasn't talking bout me. I didn't say shit else for the remainder of the ride. I bobbed my head to my music and sped home.

17

CHASTITY

While Legend was getting his daughter out the car I headed to the front door and crossed my arms over one another. I was mad I had to wait for him to unlock the door because I didn't want to stand near this nigga. He had me messed up for real. I was growing tired of all his little bitches. Fighting over a nigga was something I never did but when that girl swung on me I had to defend myself. When he claimed me as his girl and made it seem like Makalah was mines and his together that shit had me feeling good inside. However, that girl assaulting me wasn't cool.

WHEN HE OPENED THE DOOR, I stormed into what I now called my bedroom. Shit, I had been with him for months now and it didn't look like I was leaving anytime soon. I don't know what was happening between us but this nigga had my head spinning. I was slowly falling for him and now that Makalah was here she only complicated things more. This girl was heaven sent and the most adorable child ever. The way she clung to me warmed me but only if she knew I wasn't her father's girlfriend. I was simply a prisoner that I knew he would soon get rid of.

Walking into the room, I plopped down on the bed. I could hear Legend walking down the hall; I was sure he was gonna go lay Makalah down because she had fallen asleep during the ride. Deciding to go take a shower, I lifted from the bed and began running the water. I then headed into the room and stripped out my clothes throwing them inside the hamper that Lumida would be collecting this Friday.

STEPPING INTO THE SHOWER, I let the hot water soothe me. I had the water so hot the entire bathroom was foggy. *Ouch*. I flinched because my arm was in pain. I let the water run onto it in hopes it would feel better. I hadn't had a fight in years so I knew this was why it pained me. After standing under the water for some time I finally decided to lather my towel and soap up. I began washing my body from head to toe then rinsed off and washed up once more before stepping out. I pulled the fluffy white towel from the towel rack and began to dry off. I grabbed the towel I had used yesterday to wrap my hair up in it. When I opened the door I nearly jumped out my skin because Legend was sitting on the bed like a damn creep. Ignoring his presence, I walked over to the bed and pulled back the sheets. The moment I climbed in bed Legend stood to his feet and walked closer to me.

"You gone fix that fucking attitude Chas. You act like this shit my fault."

"It is your fault. You need to learn how to control your bitches *cousin*." I shot sarcastically.

"Man that ain't my bitch." he chuckled bypassing the *cousin* part.

"So you mean to tell me you ain't never fucked her?" I looked at him daring him to lie.

"Yeah I fucked both them bitches but what that mean."

"Exactly. You fucked them but I'm the one out here fighting. You ain't even my nigga and I got bitches coming for me."

"I'mma handle that hoe, don't trip."

"Sure. And what about the other bitch? I can tell sooner or later she's gonna be a problem too."

"What about her, shit? And man she ain't gone be shit."

"Exactly what the fuck I'm talking bout." I spewed and turned to my side.

"Man, what the fuck you want me to do, tell her you my bitch?! Huh? Cause if that's what you want I'll call her!" he screamed upset.

When I ignored his question he ran over to me and snatched the covers off me. My towel unraveled and exposed my naked body. His eyes wandered over every last part of me lustfully. I was sure he forgot what he was about to say. The room fell silent briefly until he demanded me to come to him. I climbed out the bed hesitantly. My anger had went away and I was now nervous. I stood in front of him naked with my nipples pointing right at him. He took a step closer to me and I could feel his penis growing in his shorts.

IN ONE SWIFT MOVE, he picked me up and carried me over to the dresser. Sitting me down, he began kissing me like it would be our last. This kiss wasn't like the first kiss we shared; this time it was more fire burning between us. That same throbbing feeling began to thumb between my legs and now I understood what it meant; I was horny as hell.

LEGEND BEGAN to place kisses on my neck then trailing down to my breast. Again my head began to spin with confusion because my body had submissively surrendered to him. Although my legs slightly shook nervously, it's like I wanted him to continue. Reading my mind, he did. His head trailed down to my tunnel and he slightly lifted my legs. When he bent down on his knees I had a feeling what he was gonna do. It wasn't really what I expected because I never experienced a man putting his tongue in between my thighs but I waited with anticipation.

. . .

HE PARTED my lips and his tongue slowly went up my slit making my legs tremble uncontrollably. He latched his mouth onto my clitoris and began sucking on it. With every lick my body jumped not being able to take it. It's like I had become sensitive down there. Flinching, and swarming, I began moaning in my cry-like voice. After a few moments of him doing this it began to feel good and my body relaxed. When I grabbed his head, he looked up at me satisfied he had me where he wanted me. He began doing something with his tongue that only lasted for a short time because I grabbed his head to make him stop just as a gush of water shot from inside me making me scream like I was dying. The feeling was so good. Actually, it was too damn good. I had never experienced nothing like it.

When Legend lifted up from the ground, he pulled me into his arms and carried me over to the bed. I was sure he wasn't done and this was the part where my nervousness came rushing back. He laid me all the way down and again he began to trace my body with kisses. As he did this he was unbuckling his shorts. He stood up to pull his briefs down then pulled his shirt over his head. Now, my legs began to tremble harder. So hard I couldn't concentrate on all his sexiness. Legend's body was so damn bomb he would make any girl lust over him. Just looking at his rock hard penis I understood why all the women were going crazy.

"Le...Lege." my words were caught up. I wanted to tell him we couldn't do this but I was scared. I wanted him to want me so I didn't want to disappoint him by saying no. I wanted so bad to blurt out that I was scared. My body had been violated without my consent and I was a unexperienced girl; However, nothing came out. Before I knew it he was coming towards me with his dick standing at attention.

Legend began stroking himself as he watched me alluringly. He placed his head at my opening and tried to force himself in. My tunnel was still dripping wet so I guess he assumed it would be easy for him to fit. However, that wasn't the case because I was a damn virgin.

"Damn this pussy tight Chas." he breathed hard like he was out of breath. When he tried to force himself in, I let out one of those cry moans. I was trying hard to be a big girl and not let my emotions get the best of me so I let him continue. I was having flashes of all those years and I couldn't hold back any more. Tears began to run down my face making Legend stop and look at me.

"I'm hurting you ma?" he asked concerned. I shook my head no so he continued. Finally getting himself inside, I felt like my insides was being split open. The room was silent except for the wetness of my vagina and the weeps that fell from my lips.

"This shit feel like heaven Chas." he bit his bottom lip and found his rhythm.

After a moment, the pain subsided and finally I was able to relax. I wrapped my arms around his neck and pulled him into me. Trying hard to get into it, I kissed him with so much passion I knew after this I was gonna be like a strung out junkie. I already loved the hell out of Legend even when I wasn't supposed to. All day, every day I thought of him. When I slept at night in this bed alone, I would try to envision what he was doing in the next room.

"Ohhhh Legend...ohhh shit baby!" a warm and sharp feeling began to run through my body. I held onto his neck for dear life. "Ummmm...shit."

"Let it out baby." he continued to stroke me. "Let it go ma." he spoke in a easy tone that was turning me on. "What we gone do after this ma? Huh? Is this gonna be mines?"

I wanted to answer every question he asked but the feeling was so great my mouth was in an O shape but no words came out. "You gone be mines Chas. I don't know how, but you gone be mines lil baby." he said and began pumping harder.

"Oh my god. Oh my god! I love you Legend." I burst out into tears. He looked at me while slowing down his pace. He studied my face confused then leaned into me to kiss my tears away.

"I'm bout to put my love child inside of you." he whispered and before I knew it his body began jerking and his dick was like it had grew more. My insides locked around him and again that heated feeling came back. My legs trembled and another gush of water rushed from inside of me. Legend let out a growl right when that gush came and I guess this was what people referred to as cumming together. Legend continued to pump, and I could feel his dick softening. He was breathing hard like he ran a race, and I guess I sounded like him because I was trying hard to catch my breath also.

"YO ASS AIN'T NEVER GOING NOWHERE." Legend said as he rolled off of me and laid back on the pillow. I turned to face him and lifted to lay my head on his chest. Thinking bout what I had just done made my emotions come rushing back. *Damn,* I thought, because my tears had fell onto his chest.

"You regret giving yourself to me?" Legend's voice brought me from my thoughts.

"It's a long story."

"I got nothing but time." he said mocking me.

"Please, I don't wanna talk about it. But to answer your question, no I don't regret it."

"So why didn't you tell me you were a virgin?"

"I don't know." I shrugged my shoulders.

"I'm just confused because the night I came in there you were..."

"We didn't do anything. Well, we didn't get a chance." I replied thinking about that night. Something told me had giving myself to Keyon wouldn't have been magical like now. Although I was having horrible memories I tried to shake them and focus on the cloud I was riding on.

18

LEGEND

The next morning I was up bright and early because it was time I handled this nigga Allen. After what happened last night with me and Chas I felt kinda bad but it had to get done. Now that we had took things further, I wondered if she would forgive me. Just thinking bout last night had a nigga in deep thought. Lil baby had the best pussy on earth, god damn my dick was getting hard thinking bout it. I couldn't believe she made a nigga talk during sex; couldn't no bitch do that. It's like with Chas, there was a crazy chemistry between us. And to me chemistry was better than sex. What bothered me was I don't know if she felt guilty about giving herself to me because she cried the entire night. I don't know if it was her dad, or ex-nigga she was missing but I could tell something pained her. Right now, I didn't have time to focus on her. I was gonna get to the bottom of it sooner or later.

WALKING into the living room where Chas was sitting at the table with her face buried into her books, I stopped to admire her. Her wild hair was all over the place as she flipped to the next page. Feeling my presence she looked up at me and a small smile crept up on her face. Her light brown eyes beamed as she watched me until I reached her.

"Hey." her voice alone sent a chill through a nigga body. I wrapped my arms around her and kissed her on the neck.

"Sup lil baby. How's yo work going?"

"I'm almost done." she replied and closed her book. "Legend, I really need to ummm...I..I need to go to school. Please don't be mad. This is my last year so I really don't wanna miss out. Summer break is coming in two weeks. I just need to at least take a few tests. It will help my grades."

For a minute, I didn't say shit. Keepin' it real I really didn't know what to say.

"Can I trust you?" I asked looking in her eyes. That once hatred stare was now replaced with lust. I knew just by the look she was falling in love with me, therefore, I knew I could trust her. However, I wanted to hear what she had to say.

"I trusted you enough to give myself to you." when she said that I nodded once because she was right.

"You right." I looked at her. "I'll have a jet fly you in.

"It's only a five hour drive. Won't that cost you a lot."

"I'm the plug baby, money ain't shit. You'll find that out soon."

"And how is that?"

"Because sooner or later I'mma spoil the fuck out of you. I just need you to love a nigga and act like Jesus." she shot me a look confused. I headed for the door but before I walked out I turned to look at her. "God forgive me for my sins." she looked at me with those same fearful eyes, except this time they were more pleasant. She may have known what I meant but if she didn't she would soon find out.

You don't know *what the fame took*
   Ain't been on the land in like two years
   Why they got me in the gang book?
   But I ride with the same hood

. . .

ZIG ZAGGING through traffic I let Lil Durk *Treacherous* spill through my speakers. I headed for the slaughter where Allen was tied up and ready to be tortured. I thought about Chas the entire way there but right now I couldn't let my emotions cloud my judgement. I needed to get this shit done and over with so I could move on with my life. I was gonna make this nigga tell me whoever he sold my shit to because they would have to pay as well.

PULLING INTO MY NORMAL SPOT, I hit Kill to let him know I was here. I headed inside and straight for the Black Hole. Flicking on the light, I walked in and sure enough Allen was tied from head to feet.

"Wakeup old man." I strutted over to him and picked up his chin that was resting on his chest. His eyes shot open and they grew wide. "Damn you look surprised. I taunted him.

"Is she okay?" he asked and it surprised the hell out of me.

"Nigga don't worry bout her now."

"Mannn, you've had your share with killing kids."

I stopped in my tracks and looked over him. His grey hairs on his head and the way he spoke told me he didn't care his life was over. He didn't have that same frantic voice he had on Chas's voicemail.

"This how we gone do this." I pulled the chair up and took a seat in front of him. I ignored his statement about killing kids although it struck a nerve. See, Allen knew all about the past that haunted me because he was around to witness it. The nigga I went to chase about my bread worked for me in the slaughter. Allen was the one around when he had ran off with my bread. Not only that but he was also the one I confided in with the information because he helped me clean up the mess I made. I came back to the slaughter that day with the gun in hand and I was in a frantic. I was so depressed I locked myself up in the office sick. Allen was on the clock that late night and it's like he could tell something was bothering me. The specks of blood on my clothing told it all and like I said he cleaned it up.

He walked in and asked for the gun. Not what happened, no nothing. I looked up at him and handed him the gun. After that I never heard a peep from him and I stayed out his way. I think this was another reason I hated him. Nobody but Kill knew what I had done and then here came Allen. A part of me felt like I owed him but because he was such a fuck nigga I always ruled against him.

"You stole from me you die. Now, Chastity she's good. That little sexy thang gone be my wife one day. Too bad you won't be here to walk her down the aisle." I snickered.

"You don't touch her you son of a bitch. That girl got a life ahead of her."

"Nigga, you don't give a fuck about her life ahead!" I jumped up from my seat. "I fucked the shit out of her last night and that shit was good. After I kill you, I'mma be fucking up in her on a regular." his eyes bucked with hatred. *Damn, Chas look just like this nigga.* I thought eyeing him.

"Well if you kill me you gotta kill yo boy too." he said and I froze. I knew he couldn't have been talking bout Kill so I listened further. "Don't look like that. You thought I did this on my own. Hell nah; since the first day this shit was plotted."

"Man who the fuck you talkin bout?"

"Brandon." he spoke with a smirk. My head cocked in his direction so hard it nearly popped off.

"Fuck you talkin bout?"

"Yo boy Bee. Yeah, he the one wanted this done so if you kill me kill his snake ass too. He paid me a great penny for this one. Why you lookin like that. You didn't know? Ha." he taunted me. "That sweet little pussy y'all both in love with, I can't wait to get my mouth on her. What's her name? Ummm... Arian, yeah her." he spoke to himself like a deranged man. But hearing him say this had my antennas up. I hadn't seen Brandon in years and how the hell would he know about Arian.

"So you trying to say Brandon set this up and Arian fucking him?"

"Arian ain't no damn saint. She been fucking him for years. How you think she knew to come to the hotel that day he set you up with his ol lady. Man you ain't as smart as you think. Guess yo dick ain't that good." he began chuckling like he was getting a kick out this shit.

. . .

SHAQ: she getting in the car with 12.

I LOOKED own at my phone just as I was about to reply to Allen. That same pain mixed with anger rushed through my body. When I say I was totally side tracked, I was stuck. Shaq was referring to Chas getting in the car with the police. Just as I read the text Kill came through the door.

"Nigga peep this." I told him showing him my phone. He paused and looked at me now worried.

"You think she gone tell them?"

"Nah. she don't know shit. I always blindfolded her." I told a half ass lie. The last time when 12 came for Immigration, Chas wasn't blind folded because we had to rush out. Something inside of me told me she didn't know where we were, and I hoped like hell she didn't pay that much attention. "I gotta get her back. And this time she dies." I looked at Kill.

"How you gone do that?"

"Shit, she love this nigga. Grab the bolt pistol." I thought quickly. Kill ran over to the corner where we keep the pistol. It was a gun-like utensil that we used to electrocute the animals before we slaughtered them. We also used it to torture humans when needed.

WE STOOD in front of Allen ready to make him scream out. Kill hit him with the bolt, while I recorded his cries. I recorded for about 30 seconds then brought the phone to my mouth. "If you wanna save yo poor little daddy I suggest you ditch the pigs." I spoke into the phone. See one thing I was certain of, was, Chas had a heart. She loved her pops unlike him. The way she tried to surrender her life for her pops, shid and that fuck boy, I knew she was loyal to them.

"Nigga, how you know that's gonna work?"

"Man trust me. That girl love the fuck out his dirtbag ass." I spoke and kicked his chair across the room. I had so much anger built up in me his body was like a feather. I couldn't believe Chas had crossed a nigga. I guess that's what I get for going against my better judgement. I shook my head just thinking bout how foolish I was. Just when I thought she loved a nigga, she crossed me. I just prayed my plan worked and she would come for her father as I expected. Both, Chas and Allen were gonna be dead and all this shit would be over.

"It's yo lucky fucking day old man." I snarled and headed for the door. I took one last look at Allen then walked out in a rage.

"We were at my house and we went to grab something to eat. While we were in the car waiting for our food some guys ran up to our vehicle and pointed guns at us demanding we get out. They threw us into a van and drove us for nearly two days. The last sign I saw was Mexico City. When we arrived they took Keyon one way and me the other."

"So you were in Mexico City and what they do to you this entire time?"

"The entire time I was there they raped me and beat me. There was a leader I vividly remember his face. He instructed them on what to do. The entire time he spoke on Keyon owing him some money."

"And during the time of you dating Keyon have he indulged in any illegal activities?"

"I'm not sure but he was always on the phone. He had nice things and anything I said I wanted he bought. If he was, he wouldn't tell me because I and his mother are really close. He calls me a snitch because I report to her how he fails in schools."

"So after you were let go where did you go?"

"Ummm...I walked for hours. I was in the middle of nowhere. Finally a big rig truck pulled over. I climbed in and he gave me a lift out to I-10 East. from there I caught another ride and that's how I ended up here. Can I call my father? I know he's worried about me?"

"Your father isn't answering. We called him several times. His number was registered as your emergency contact."

"Well, have you guys spoken to Mrs. McCoy? Is Keyon okay? Please tell me he's okay?" I put on my award winning act.

"We're sorry but we have no signs or traces of Mr. McCoy."

"What?" I asked like I was in shock. I dropped my head into my arms and began to cry my heart out. The officers rushed to my side and began consoling me. After a little while of my act I lifted my head up to speak. "I'm scared. I'm scared to stay here. What if they come after me again?" I began to sob.

"You'll be okay Ms. Roberts. Do you have friends or family you can go stay with for a while?."

"No." I shook my head. I sat back because I knew I had them. They told me I could leave and I felt relieved. A part of me felt horrible but after everything I've experienced with Legend I couldn't bring myself to tell on him.

WALKING out of the station I was met with Mera and Nancy. Mera stood with a blanket wrapped around her which was evident they had been here a long time. Nancy ran over to me and hugged me tightly. Hugging her back I eyed Mera infuriated. I let go of Nancy and walked up on Mera. She extended her arms as if she expected a hug. Instead, I gave her a hug alright. I punched her ass so hard she flew into the red Dodge Charger that was parked alongside the curb.

"Chastity!" Nancy called my name astonished.

"I'll explain it later." I told Nancy still mugging Mera who held her jaw surprised. I hopped into the taxi that awaited me. I had the taxi take me to the same location they had picked me up which was the lot the Jet had landed on.

AS I BOARDED THE JET, I asked the man to use his phone to call

Legend. He handed me the phone and instead I called my phone so I could check my messages. The first message was from Mrs. McCoy just as I expected. I only had two more messages so I figured Legend had deleted the other ones. As I began to listen to the next message, I nearly jumped out my seat. It was a message from an unknown number but my father's screams were vivid. Tears began to roll down my eyes and I now felt like shit. The man that I was falling in love with was gonna murder my flesh and blood. I laid back in the seat and began pondering on where could they be and why would he leave me a message. *The Slaughter.* I thought knowing they had him there. Thanks to the last time we had to flee, I remembered exactly where the location was. When the jet landed, I was going straight there in hopes to talk Legend out of killing my father. If I had to pay back every dime then I would. I don't know how but I would.

By THE TIME I pulled up to The Slaughter, I was exhausted from the ride and my constant cries. I felt so drained that it made me wanna turn around. I wasn't mentally prepared to see what lies ahead of me. I nervously knocked on the door and was let in by an older Hispanic man. He wore some old raggedy jeans and was pushing a trash can along with a broom and other cleaning supplies. I remembered him and I was sure he remembered me because he let me in without hesitation.

Thanking him, I smiled and asked was Legend here. When he shook his head no I said okay and my eyes fell onto the many keys that hung from a thick brown belt. "Can you open door?" I asked him but he couldn't understand what I was saying. I pulled his arm and led him to what I referred to as the dungeon. I used my hands to gesture unlocking the door. "Ahhh." he replied and pulled the keys up. *Yes,* I thought as he began to open the door. "Gracias." I thanked him in my broken Spanish. He smiled and scurried away as I stepped into the door. I turned on the light and there he was tied up like a prisoner.

"Dad." I ran over to him and kneeled down in front of him.

"Chastity." he looked up at me in denial. "Baby, I'm so happy to see you. You gotta get me out of here before they kill me."

I began looking around the room but I didn't see anything to cut the rope with.

"I'll be right back. I'm gonna get you out of here okay." he nodded his head okay and I left out the dungeon to find a knife.

Looking high and low I found a box cutter. Because it was a slaughter I knew there were plenty knives inside but where they conducted the slaughtering was always too busy and I couldn't take the chance of someone seeing me. I ran back inside the dungeon and instantly began to cut the rope. Because the rope was thick it took lots of cutting and struggling but I managed to get my father untied.

"Dad, we have to get you out of here." I pulled the last part of the rope from around him. He jumped to his feet and I pulled him over to the secret passage that Legend had led me out of. I began screening the wall to find the button but I couldn't locate it. Suddenly the sound of keys could be heard so I began to panic.

"Where is it." I eagerly searched the wall. I hit something that was really small and suddenly the door came open.

"Dad you have to go. This door will lead you outside."

"Come on baby."

"No dad I can't. I'm fine; trust me. Just please go." I told him as tears poured down my face. He nodded his head once and rushed into the secret passage. I hit the button again and the door closed behind him. Just as I turned around someone came into the room. It was Legend's friend. He looked at me and I could tell he expected it to be my father. My legs began to tremble and my heart was beating so loud I was sure you could hear it through my chest. I swallowed the lump in my throat and I was sure if I didn't die last time I was dead now. However, for my father's life I would do it again.

Legend

. . .

THE SOUND of my phone ringing was beginning to distract me so I powered it off. Right now I had a mission and I couldn't get side-tracked. I sat outside of Brandon's crib out in Lawrenceville and watched him exit his whip. I shook my head at how comfortable this nigga was after he had played a part in robbing me for 2 million fucking dollars. This nigga was foul as fuck in so many ways. I thought about what Allen had said and I knew everything was the truth. How the fuck would he know about Arian? All along I'm thinking Arian found me on a iPhone app but that was bullshit. Her and Brandon had been fucking behind my back and he the one told her about me and Bianca. Just as Brandon, Arian was foul too. And this was the reason I didn't wife these scandalous ass hoes. Shit, look at Chas. She had a nigga fooled all along. Bitch went as far as to giving me her virginity and even screaming she loved me while we was fucking. All along bitch was setting me up for failure.

GRABBING MY PISTOL, I held it to the side of me and stepped out my whip. I took the few steps up to his front door and rang the bell. I ducked off to the side and I could see his shadow come to the door then disappear. Again I reached over and rung the bell then hid again. Just like I had expected he opened the door and began searching the porch.

"Surprise bitch." I stuck my gun in his face. Looking into my eyes he was finally alarmed and the muthfucka tried to run.

POP!

I SENT a shot to his leg. I could have finished him off but I didn't want it to be that easy. I closed the door behind us and stepped further into the home.

"Oh my god!" the sound of a woman's voice came into view as she kneeled down next to Brandon.

"Who else in the house?" she looked over and her eyes grew.

"Please oh my god. Please don't hurt us." she began crying. I watched her and something about her piqued my interest. She looked too familiar but I couldn't remember from where. "You can take whatever you want." she was crying hysterically. I wanted so bad to hear what Brandon had to say but the presence of the lady was distracting me. I fired a shot into his head then one into his chest making the lady jump.

"Noooooo." she was over Brandon's body with tears running down her face. "Legend please." she said making my neck pop.

"How the fuck you know my name?" I pointed my strap at her head.

"Please don't kill me. I know you because of Brandon. All he talks about is you. I've seen pictures." she said and began biting her lip. My trigger finger began to itch and I wanted to blow her brains out right along with Brandon.

I PULLED the pictures from my pocket that I had got from Eddie. Because they were taken just yesterday I couldn't get many but the ones I got were enough to make her hate him. I dropped the pictures to the ground and she began looking through them one by one. It was pictures of Brandon kissing a young, White boy inside Starbucks. The next picture was of them walking out and then another of Brandon kissing him by a car. Her eyes began roaming over the pictures. I watched her as she studied the pictures and she looked so damn familiar. She looked up at me and the tears she once had were now gone.

"This boy has been to my house." she flipped through the pictures. "He said...he said he was a co-worker."

"Well he lied." I said and stepped to the side. It was time I left but I needed to finish the job. Leave no witnesses is what I constantly practice and after the shit Chastity had pulled I had to rid this lady. Or so I thought....my eyes fell onto a picture that sat on a old record player. It was the same lady that was right here and she was hugging a small child. I looked from the picture to the lady then back to the picture. *It's her.* I thought as my heart began to pump. I watched her for a moment and it all came back to me. That same pain I felt years ago had resurfaced and I couldn't bring myself to kill her.

"Are you gonna kill me?" she asked petrified. Feeling rueful I shook my head no. I couldn't bring myself to doing it. This was the second time we crossed paths and I had already brought enough grief into this woman's life.

"It's your lucky day. Normally I leave no witnesses but I'm trusting you on this one. Tell them it was a break-in." I walked over to the door and used my gun to bust open the window. I shot the lady one last look and headed out with the world on my shoulders. I climbed into my whip and laid my head back for a split second. Finally being able to get ahold of myself I drove towards my crib with so much on my mind. The life I was living was finally starting to weigh heavy on me. Shit was becoming too stressful and sooner or later something was gonna have to change.

20

LEGEND

Looking at the sketch of the mask described in my mother's killing I clutched a bottle of Hennessy tightly. I took swig after swig to numb the pain I was feeling. I don't why I done it to myself but anytime things were on my mind I would look at the sketch given to my pops by the police. I also had another one that I used for target practice because one day I would get my chance.

Dropping the paper onto the dinner table, I let out a deep sigh and took another swig. I don't know if I was blocking my blessings with all the shit I had done in my life or what, but shit just wasn't working out for me. One would think with all the paper I had that shit would be looking up for me. Instead, I had 99 problems and a bitch was 1. There was Chas, then her pops, then here comes the shit with Brandon and now this. The lady that was in Brandon's crib was the same lady whose son I had murdered years ago and that's why I couldn't bring myself to kill her. When she said my name I figured she knew me from that but it was impossible. Brandon didn't know about that situation because we weren't friends at the time.

It was puzzling to me how he hooked up with her but you know what they say, small world. Speaking of Brandon, it didn't surprise me when Eddie gave me those pics of him and the boy. That nigga was always weird as fuck to me. A normal teenage boy wanted nothing but pussy and money. However, Brandon always locked himself in a room full of niggas playing 2k. He would go to movies with nothing but guys and anytime I went around him when we were younger he was always around a bunch of niggas.

Growing up, I wasn't much of a people person so I kept my distance whenever he had a crowd around. When he got with Bianca, it was because of me. She was checking him out and the nigga almost didn't even wanna get at her. When I called him a pussy and asked was he gay he got offended and got her number.

LOOKING at my phone that sat on the table in front of me I decided to power it on. I had a shit load of messages from Kill and Megan. I went to Megan's text and began reading.

MEGAN: she put me out and I don't have nowhere to go

Megan: Buck please I'm out in the cold. She put me out weeks ago and I been staying with my friend who now wants me gone.

Megan: If you can at least give me some money to get a hotel

IGNORING Megan's text I went to Kill.

K: nigga I need you to call me asap (code red)

SEEING his message I quickly hit send on his number and called him. He answered on the third ring and I could tell this shit was serious.

"Nigga you ain't gone believe this shit. Allen gone."

"Fuck you mean he gone?" I jumped to my feet.

"Man. Chastity ass let the nigga go. And trip this, she used yo secret tunnel."

. . .

1,2,3,4.. I tried my normal breathing tactic because I felt myself about to lose it. 5,6,7...the more I counted the angrier I became. Before I knew it, I lost it. I started tearing up the house because Chas wasn't right here for me to take it out on her. I slammed my chair into the glass table and after that I went into a rage.

"Legend Mijo!" the sound of Lumida's voice brought me to. She ran over to my side and began rubbing my back. "Noooo. It's okay Mijo; it's okay." she tried to calm me down. Lumida knew about my attacks and because my mother was no longer here she was the only one that could calm me down.

"Legend!" Lumida and I looked at the phone and Kill was screaming my name through the receiver. I had blanked the fuck out that I forgot I was even on the phone.

"Bring that bitch to me." I roared into the phone and hung up because there was nothing else to say. I grabbed the bottle of Hennessy and headed outside to get some air. I could feel Lumida's eyes watching me because she knew like I knew when I got like this I was capable of anything.

WATCHING the headlights that shined brightly through my picture window, Lumida jumped to her feet and ran to open the door. Since my episode she hadn't moved an inch. The entire time she sat in the chair across from me sewing what looked like a baby sweater as I continued to drink my Henn. Hearing the car doors slam I became impatient. Because I had destroyed my table I had my strap on the chair on the side of me. When Kill walked in, his huge frame covered Chas little body. Kill looked around but he already knew what happened. When Chas stepped into view I could tell she had been crying from the white traces of tears. She had one hand in the other as she stood there looking nervous. I looked at her through a pair of cold, black eyes and the minute I thought of what she had done sent me into another rage. I dashed at her so fast I used all the power I had inside of me and slapped her so hard she flew back into the door.

"I'm sorry!" she screamed out as tears filled her face in an instant. Sorry wasn't good enough. I wrapped my hands around her throat and began squeezing so hard the veins in her neck popped out.

"Legend nooo, please mijo!" Lumida held my arms trying to get me off her. Kill ran over and grabbed Lumida as she began to cry. He pulled her out the room and led her down the hall.

"Le..Lege..Legend please. I'm sorry!" she cried out as her nails dug into my wrist.

"Oh you wanna scratch bitch?" I jumped up and went to grab my gun. I pointed it at her and her eyes grew with fear. "Give me reason I shouldn't blow yo fucking brains out." she looked from my strap back to me and her eyes held so much sorrow.

"Chastity." I heard Makalah tiny voice. I looked over and she looked scared.

"Go to bed Kalah!" I shouted making her jump. She didn't move until she heard Chas voice.

"I'm okay Makalah." Chas let out a faint smile. Makalah backed away with fear still in her eyes and she disappeared.

"I didn't tell the police anything. That's how I ended up back. They took me for questioning and let me go so I took the jet back to the slaughter. Legend, I love you. I wasn't gonna leave you." she whimpered as she brought me from my daze.

I knew there was some truth behind it because how did she end up at the slaughter and not to mention the police would have come by now. But that still didn't justify what she had done.

"I told you I was gonna kill that nigga and you decided to stay with me. How the fuck you gone pay 2 million fucking dollars?"

"I don't know but I'll try Legend, please." she grabbed my arm and fell into my chest crying. Just hearing her say she didn't tell the cops on me made me calm down a bit but her letting her pops go was something I couldn't swallow.

"Fuck off me." I shoved her off me. "Get the fuck out my face before I end yo life." I told her and she looked at me before leaving.

Her face frowned and it was evident she was sorry. I had to turn away from her because I nearly gave in. After a faint pause, I could hear her feet turn to walk away. Finally looking in her direction, I watched as she stormed down the hall. Moments later, Kill came back into the room and just stared at me.

"You straight my nigga?"

"Yeah, I'm good. I just can't believe her dumb ass."

"I mean, what you expect, shit? Its' her pops. But check it, Carlos the one let her in. I asked him how she ended up there and he said she came by herself. Now I can't justify for her actions with her pops but that chick in love with you. I mean, it's clear. She didn't tell the police because they would have had the slaughter or yo crib surrounded. Don't worry bout Allen. I got a manhunt on him. You just figure shit out with her." his eyes shot down the hall.

He walked towards the door and before he walked out his eyes roamed around the mess I had made. "Nigga you still throwing tantrums and shit like you twelve. Clean this shit up." he said and walked out. I slightly chuckled because he repeated what my pops always said. I let out a sigh because I had finally calmed down. I looked over the mess and walked out leaving that shit as is. I was gonna have Lumida order a new table and hire someone to clean the glass up tomorrow.

As I headed down the hall to my room, I could hear light weeps seeping from under Chas door. I stopped to listen for a moment and each minute that past I felt worse. Never in my life had I put my hands on a woman so right now I was regretting it. I wanted so bad to go inside and tell her I apologized but truthfully she deserved it. It could have been worse.

Walking into my bedroom, Makalah was wide awake sitting up in my bed. Again I began to feel bad. She was watching my every move as I roamed around my room. I grabbed some pajama pants from my drawer and went into the restroom to change. I decided to just shower tomorrow so I climbed into bed with my baby.

"Daddy is Chastity okay?" she asked concerned.

"Yeah baby ,she okay."

"Is she still gonna be my mommy?" she asked shocking the hell out of me.

"Denise is your mother, baby, but yes Chastity is still gonna be your other mommy." I replied. No matter how foolish Denise had been by just dropping her off, I wasn't gonna just say fuck her. She had raised Makalah by herself for years so I at least owed her that much.

"Can I go sleep with her?" she asked and lifted from the bed before I could say yes. I nodded my head and her eyes lit up with excitement. My baby loved Chas like her own mother and after tonight it was evident. Damn, I was in trouble and I had to figure this shit out. However, I was gonna make Chas suffer because right now, I wasn't fucking with lil baby.

21

CHASTITY

3 DAYS LATER

For the last 3 days Legend and I walked around the house not saying much to each other. Anything I would ask he would snap at me so I decided to keep my distance. I spent these days pretty much cooped up in my room with my head buried in my books. The only thing I had to keep me sane was Makalah and Lumida. Yesterday, Lumida had brought me my phone but I didn't bother to turn it on. I wanted so bad to get on social media or even call Nancy but I decided not to. I felt like enemy of the state because of the guilt from Keyon. I didn't wanna have to explain where I been and I wasn't ready to explain to Nancy why I did what I did to Mera.

"Chastity." Makalah called out to me bringing me from my thoughts.

"Yes sweety?"

"Can you get me some water? I'm thirsty."

"Sure, just make sure you use the bathroom before you go back to sleep."

"Okay." she replied.

I lifted from the bed and headed out the door. I went into the kitchen and grabbed a bottled water and headed back for my room. I wanted so bad to go into Legend's room and climb into bed with him but I was too damn scared because the way he had been treating me. I stood there for a split second and decided to give it a try. I headed down to Legend's door nervously. I stood at his door to listen for any sounds of movement and something more intense grabbed my attention. The sound of a woman's voice could be heard followed by a soft moan. Curiously, I pushed the door open and sure enough there was a woman on top of him. The sheet barely covered her ass as Legend held on tightly to her ass cheeks. I stood there frozen for a split second with my heart literally on the floor. The gasp from my voice made them both turn around. The girl watched me and tried to grab the blanket to cover up. However, Legend smirked like the shit was premeditated for me to see.

With tears streaming down my face I ran out the room embarrassed. I climbed into the bed with Makalah and tried hard to hide my tears. She was already snuggled under the blanket so I figured she was on her way to sleep. Or so I thought.

"Don't cry Chastity. Daddy loves you." she said not facing me. Just hearing her say those words made me cry harder. Just thoughts of Legend sharing his bed with another woman hurt. What hurt worse was he didn't care that I was here. I mean, I understood this was his home but it was straight up disrespectful. Yeah, it was time for me to go. I don't know how because my father was still on the loose but I was gonna try. This man was bringing back that same tainted pain from my past so I had to get away from him.

THE NEXT MORNING, I opened my eyes feeling like shit. My body was drained and I was feeling like I was at the end of my ropes. I climbed out of bed and went into the restroom and handled my hygiene. Looking in the mirror, I couldn't do anything but shake my head. It wasn't even the small gash from Legend's smack across the face that saddened me; it was the hurt and pain in my eyes from loving a man that I was supposed to hate. I thought back to the day I caught Keyon kissing that girl and not even that pain amount to this. Shit, even when I saw the pictures of he and Mera kissing, it didn't affect me as much as right now. I was coming to terms with myself that God was punishing me for falling in love with Legend. However, after today, I was gonna push my feelings aside and convince him to let me go.

AFTER I WAS DONE, I headed out the room and down the hall in search for Legend. I pushed the thoughts out my mind so he wouldn't see that he had gotten to me. I was tired of being weak for him. Last night was the last time I cried over any man. I walked into the den and he was laid back on the phone. His leg was kicked over the arm of the sofa and the smile on his face was evident it was a woman. When he looked up at me, his eyes held pure hatred. It's crazy because he used to look at me like I was the most enticing woman on earth.

"Stacy, let me hit you back ma." he said into the phone not caring that I was standing there.

"I think it's best if I just leave. I'll get a job on campus and pay you all your money back." he looked at me shocked by what I said and instead of the reaction I was hoping for, he looked at me again with that same look.

"Bye, what's stopping you." he responded irately. Without another word, I headed towards my room and began packing the few belongings I had. Once I was done I walked back into the living area struggling with my bags.

"Chas, you leaving?" Makalah ran towards me.

"Yes baby. I have to go."

"You coming back?" she asked looking over my bags.

Legend walked into view and called her name but she didn't budge.

"No baby." I replied dying inside.

"But I don't want you to leave."

"Makalah, go in yo room."

"No daddy please. Please don't let Chastity leave me. Please!" she burst out into tears. The look on Legend's face told me he was a bit hurt but as for me I was dismal. It tore me up inside seeing Makalah crying over me. I looked at Legend one last time with glossy eyes but I quickly turned to walk away before my tears fell. The moment I hit the porch I closed the door behind me. I could still hear the sounds of Makalah's cries and I couldn't hold back the tears. As I walked out into his yard a hurting pain shot through my body making me drop to my knees. I sat in this one spot and cried like a baby. I was beyond hurt.

Legend

I PEERED out my window as Chas sat on her knees crying her eyes out. I wanted so bad to run to her side and tell her the truth, that, I didn't want her to leave. I wanted her to stay and we could figure this shit out. However, my pride was too big. I knew this girl loved me and the way she was crying right now confirmed it more than ever. Not being able to take seeing her like this I had to move from the window and go get Lumida. I also told Lumida to give her $500 so she could get to school and have money to eat. I knew Chas didn't have a dime on her so it was the least I could do. I already felt like I had gave her my ass to kiss and she really didn't deserve it.

WHEN SHE WALKED into the room on me fucking Stacy I had done it purposely. I expected her to get mad and just walk out but instead the shit backfired. When she told me it was best she left again, my pride made me react like I didn't care. Really, I called myself calling her bluff. When she walked out the room holding her bags the shit shocked the fuck out of me. I was hoping Makalah's tears would help and she would stay but that was wishful thinking. Not even her baby could make her stay which told me she really wanted to get the fuck away from me.

I ain't gone lie, a nigga almost shed a tear when I watched her through that window. Just that fast I was feeling all empty and shit without her. I didn't give a fuck about her working to pay off her pops' debt. Shit, I wanted my girl back. I always believed the saying God put people in your life for a reason, either they a lesson or a blessing. Shit, Chastity was both. Her and Makalah had both come into my life at the same time making me feel slightly whole. The only reason I didn't feel completely whole was because Chas and I had to figure shit out to make *us* official. That girl was indeed a blessing and I guess my lesson learned was never let my pride cloud my heart.

A part of me told me that I would always have a space in my heart just for her. As bad as I wanted to, I had to let her go. That girl had an entire future and I was only gonna hold her back. So maybe it was best she left.

I HEADED into my bedroom and Makalah was laying on my bed asleep. My baby had cried herself into a nap over Chas. I felt bad because the pain I brought Makalah was all my fault. I placed a kiss on her forehead and whispered in her ear "Daddy sorry." I truly was. I headed into the room to tell Lumida keep an eye on her so I could head out. A nigga needed to get some air and get his mind right.

JUMPING into my whip I turned on my Makaveli CD. I went to this particular song and turned my music up as I headed for my destination.

ME AND YOU *against the world, we untouchable*
   Screamin' like you dyin' every time I'm fuckin' you
   Ya never had a father or a family, but I'll be there
   No need to fear so much insanity, and through the years
   I know ya gave me your heart, plus
   When I'm dirt broke and fucked up, ya still love me

. . .

PULLING up to Kill's crib I had played the song three times. I was hoping he wasn't outside because he was gonna talk shit about my choice of music. He knew me all too well to know I wasn't no lovey dovey type nigga. I hopped out the car and headed to his door. It was a Sunday afternoon so I was sure he was home. Every Sunday was what Kill called family day. He would spend time with his girl and two kids.

"Hey Legend." Patrice said opening the door.

"Hey Trice." I smiled and walked in. "Where yo boy at?"

"He's in his man cave." she used her hands to gesture quotations.

Chuckling, I headed down the hall and down the steps into the basement. Every time I walked into this nigga crib it was always so peaceful. It was crazy how this nigga did so much dirt in the streets with a family like he had. His kids were cool and bright with good educations. Trice was mad cool too. She held that nigga down and I respected her for that. I always said the day I got married I wanted a life like Kills.

"SUP FOO." we pounded fists. Just as I was taking a seat Patrice came in and passed me a Heineken.

"Thanks ma." I took the beer and got comfortable on the lazy boy chair.

"You ever think about leaving the game?" I asked him getting right to it.

"Hell nah. Why you ask that though?"

"Shit, I don't know. I guess cause yo family. You got a good ass wife and some dope ass kids. If you wanna leave you got my blessings."

"Nigga, either you bumped your head or Chas got you gone gone." we both laughed. "Nah but real shit I feel you. I think about it sometimes but I don't wanna just leave you in the game alone my nigga. We built a empire together so I'll leave when you leave." I nodded my head and respected his answer. I really couldn't argue with him because he was right. We built this shit together. Although my pops had left me a business, Kill had been by a nigga side through the coke sales. We both were sitting on millions of dollars and I owed this nigga my life. He's the one that handled the bread, collected from the spot and made sure my account stayed fat. We were closer than homies, more like brothers and he was the only person I felt I could really trust.

"What's up with Chas?" he asked bringing me from my daze.

"She left."

"What you mean?"

"Shit, I let her go. I fucked Stacy last night and she walked into the room on us. Shit, she woke up this morning and decided to leave a nigga." I shrugged like it was okay. But deep inside it wasn't.

"Nigga, you let her leave? And why the fuck would you do that? Man, you crazy. You betta get yo girl back. Girls like Chastity only come a dime a dozen. At first it was all fun and games but when she got picked up by 12 and didn't tell on us nigga I knew then she was down for yo funny looking ass." I nodded my head because I couldn't say shit; he was right. Like always. "So where she go back to school?"

"Yep. And man Makalah went crazy." I thought about the way my baby was screaming.

"Yeah?" he asked surprised. "Makalah fucks with Chas. That's dope."

"Was dope. It's over now. Makalah gone be alright." I took a swig from my beer.

"Nah nigga she ain't. Her sorry ass mama basically abandoned her. That little girl found a mother in Chas. She needs that. Lumida sure in the hell ain't no mother. Grandma yes, mother no." we both chuckled and the room fell silent. I began to ponder on what he was saying but I was too busy trying to convince myself that Chas was better off gone. We continued to wrap and the entire time I thought about her. Something in the pit of my stomach told me I wasn't gone be the same unless I got her back.

22

CHASTITY

3 MONTHS LATER...

T hey say if you love something, you've got to let it go.
And if it comes back, then it means so much more.
Fine if it never does, at least you will know,
That it was something you had to go through to grow.

"CHASTITY... CHAS!"

"Oh huh?"

"Girl, you always blanking out on me. You hungry?"

"No I'm fine."

"Well it's not for you; it's for the baby."

CLUTCHING MY SMALL ROUND BELLY, I smiled at Nancy who was always shoving food down my throat. I don't know what it was about this baby but I rarely had an appetite. Yes, you heard right. I was with child. I had found out I was pregnant a month after I left Legend's home. I wanted so bad to reach out to him but I felt like it was a waste of time. Him letting me leave showed me he didn't care so I didn't wanna make it seem like I was doing this to trap him.

I actually went to the doctor ready to get an abortion but my heart wouldn't let me do it. I was so lonely in this world. I wanted someone to love me and make me feel alive again. Since the day Legend and I parted ways I had been feeling lost. I had grown so accustomed with being in his presence it was hard. I thought of him every day, all day that sometimes I would cry myself to sleep. The baby inside of me made me feel close to him and this was another reason I decided to keep it.

"Aww, I know Keyon would be so happy." Nancy said walking into my room with a box of pizza.

I nodded my head and faintly smiled. Because I didn't want to have to explain this to the world I let everyone think the baby was Keyon's. The same story I told the police was the same story I told Nancy and Mrs. McCoy, who I finally talked to. I didn't bother to mention to Mrs. McCoy about my pregnancy because I didn't need her getting attached to a baby that wasn't her grandchild. Because of Keyon's death, I knew she would in fact want to be in the baby's life.

I HADN'T HEARD from my father since the day I let him go from the slaughter. I prayed everyday he would call so I could tell him about the baby. Guilt of the child being Legend's weighed heavy on me but my father was all I had so he deserved to know.

"Let's go to the student store." I told Nancy as she dug into her pizza.

"Oh my god, what you want, some sour patches and a Pepsi?" she laughed knowing me like a book.

"Yes and some red vines."

"Okay. I need to grab some pencils and more paper anyway."

I continued to eat and once I was done I stood to my feet and took my plate into the kitchen. I then headed into my room and grabbed my purse. Nancy and I headed out the door and I couldn't wait to get my hands on those damn red vines.

. . .

WALKING TO THE STORE, Nancy and I made small talk. Just as we neared the store, Mera was standing off to the side with a girl name Trisha. They both looked in my direction and I could tell Mera had said something about me. Not paying them any mind I headed into the store bumping right into Joseph.

"Sorry fat girl." he said and began laughing.

"It's okay Joseph. Where you off to?"

"My dorm so I could get laid." he laughed shocking the hell out of me. "My, have things changed." I laughed because I thought he would be a virgin for the rest of his life.

"Oh child you missed a lot. I'm the man around here now."

"Oh my god." I laughed so hard I almost pissed on myself.

"Ugh, he just nasty." Nancy said walking over to us. She handed me a bag filled with the candy I wanted, my Pepsi and all types of other things. When I went to reach and give her the money she declined. "Girl he didn't tell you he fucked Mera." Nancy smirked looking at Joseph.

"Mind yo business Nancy." again we all laughed. We walked out the store and began to crack jokes. It didn't surprise me because Mera was loose. She gave herself to any and everybody with a dick.

As SOON AS we walked past her I burst out into laughter. She shot me a irate look as if she knew we were talking about her.

"Joseph." she called his name and I guess she expected him to run to her side. Instead Joseph shot her a mean mug and put one finger up. Again, I began laughing and it pissed her off more. After talking to us for a few more moments he walked over to see what Mera wanted.

"You really hate her." Nancy nudged my shoulder.

"Fuck her."

"What did she do so bad?" she asked because I had never told her I found out about Mera and Keyon.

"The night Keyon and I were gonna... girl I went through his phone and found text messages between them two. I could tell he erased most of them because it started from *what you talking about.*" I began making up lie after lie about their text and Nancy's mouth hung open the entire time.

"I knew it. I told you that bitch wasn't to be trusted." Nancy shook her head and looked over in Mera's direction.

"My dad too. He always told me watch her. I never told you but she did this to me before." I went on to tell Nancy about the time I caught her getting fingered by Marcell. The entire time Nancy shook her head.

"What the fuck they looking at?" Nancy said wondering what had everyone's attention. Using my hand to block the sun, I looked up into the sky and there was a helicopter flying over the school. It was pretty low so a few people ran thinking it was gonna fall from the sky. From where we stood we had a good view of the field and that's where the helicopter hovered over. After another round, it landed. Now everyone's attention was on the pretty shiny copter. Suddenly, a man stepped out along with another man. I studied the man closely as he became more into view. *Legend.* I thought watching him walk into my direction.

When he got into arms' reach he looked me in my eyes and we held each other's gaze. When I broke eye contact, everyone around us watched in awe. My eyes fell onto Mera who stood there wondering what was going on. I looked back to Legend as butterflies began to grow in my stomach. Suddenly his eyes fell from mines and he looked down at my stomach. I instantly got nervous because his facial expression went from heavy hearted to enraged.

"Let's go Chas." his voice boomed making everyone gasp.

"I..uhh...I can't just..."

"Man bring yo ass on or I'mma drag you away." he said and walked back towards the helicopter.

"Girl who is that?" Nancy asked with a smirk.

"It's a long story." I let out a sigh. "I'll call you and explain everything to you." I told her ready to come clean. I knew I could trust Nancy so I was gonna tell her everything except Legend killing Keyon and going after my father.

. . .

WELP, there goes my Pretty Woman ending, I thought referring to Richard Greer pulling up in the limo with roses. But how could I be foolish; this was Legend the asshole. However, him demanding me to come and not only that, but him showing up in a helicopter was sexy. I turned to look at Mera and she had envy written all over her face. Smirking, I walked off towards the helicopter and was helped in by Legend's friend. The same one that was always there. When I walked on board, Legend was seated in the back looking out the window. I took a seat in the copter and it began to take off. I looked out the window and Nancy was still standing there with a huge smile plastered on her face. Knowing Nancy she was happy for me and I also knew the minute I got to my destination she was gonna be blowing up my phone.

AS THE COPTER flew through the sky the ride was smooth and the ray of the sun was breathtaking. From time to time Legend and I looked at each other but neither one of us said a word. It's like we battled with our eyes. We were basically flirting until he looked down at my belly then he would look away. I wanted so bad to tear into my red vines but I was too nervous to move. This man had some type of power over me and the feeling was crazy.

On campus, I was this free spirit girl with no worries. But around Legend I was a shy, timid girl that obeyed to his every command. He didn't demand anything from me but effortlessly my mind didn't stand a chance against my heart. I stole a glance over at him and he looked so damn good. He was looking too damn good to be in The Slaughter so I instantly got jealous. He was wearing a Givenchy top with black jeans and a pair of Givenchy shoes to match. Like always he wore his chain that had a Large L pendant and diamond earrings that was bright like the sun. He had a black cap resting on the top of his head and just watching him gave me that tingle in my inner thighs.

Legend knew he was the shit and it was evident in his walk alone. I'm mean who the hell flies around in helicopters? What puzzled me was, I didn't have shit but a textbook to my name. *What could I possibly do for a man like him? Okay Chas you're jumping the gun. Maybe he taking you back to kill you. Or maybe it's your dad. Nah that can't be. Oh shit, maybe it's the money I owe him.* I thought of all types of shit. Not once did I think of maybe he just missed me because Legend could have any women on this earth. And once again, what could he do with a chick like me that didn't have anything to offer.

23

LEGEND

From time to time I looked over at Chas and a nigga heart was thumping in my chest. Dressed simple in her little summer dress she looked pretty as fuck. I missed this girl like a muthafucka. After beating myself up for three months I had finally listened to Kill and came to get her. I was happy I did because she looked peaceful being in my presence. I could tell she was nervous about the baby but real shit, I already knew. Come on, y'all know me. Ain't no way my bitch was about to be in school and me not have Eddie watch her every move. I got pictures of the day her ass went into the doctor's off and every visit after. He also captured a few shots of her ass running into that damn student store feeding my baby all that damn junk food. Right now she thought I was upset but I was gonna play along. Y'all know I had to be an asshole for a bit.

WHEN THE HELICOPTER LANDED ,Chas got up thinking we were getting off. I grabbed her hand to let her know sit back down and she did as told. Kill stepped off the helicopter and headed for his ride. The copter pulled off and flew back into the air and headed for Tybee

Island. I looked down at my watch to make sure I was on time. The sun was setting at 5:47 PM and it was almost 5:00 now.

Lifting up from my seat I closed the curtain to separate us from Eddie who was flying us. I looked over to Chas and motioned for her to come to me. She got up from her seat and walked over to me. The helicopter was big in the inside but not tall enough for us to stand up so she had to slightly bend down. It was a Airbus AS350 so it fit three people in the back and two in the front.

I pulled her down onto my lap and as soon as she sat down my dick got hard. The pregnancy had her hips spreading and her ass got a little fatter. I pulled her hand into mines and I could see the smile that appeared on her face. Pulling her down, I kissed into her neck and she started giggling. She turned around in her seat and kissed my lips. She then laid her back against my chest and moved our hands up to her stomach. She placed mines on her little round belly and put hers on top. I closed my eyes and took in the moment.

"We bout to have a baby huh."

"Yes. I'm sorry I didn't..."

"It's alright ma. A nigga happy. But I was gone beat yo ass if you would've killed my seed." she quickly turned around shocked that I knew and sooner or later she was gone learn that I knew every muthafucka thing she did in life. "You missed a nigga?"

She turned completely around and now straddled me.

"Of course. Did you miss me is the question?"

"Like a muthafucka baby. Look, I know shit got rocky and I apologize ma. Losing you killed me every day. Chas, I know the way we connected is crazy but I fell in love with you. I guess you leaving me made me realize I couldn't live without you."

"I love you too." she cooed and looked out the window.

JUST IN TIME the sun begin to set and her eyes began to beam. I could tell she loved the setting and it was perfect for the moment. I began kissing her neck and moved my lips down to her chest. I slightly lifted her body up so I could pull her dress up to have full access to her breasts. I took them in my mouth one at a time and began teasing her hard nipples with my tongue. Her head cocked back and a soft moan escaped her lips. My dick grew in my jeans poking at the crotch of her panties.

Not being able to hold back I slid her panties to the side and began fingering her. Her pussy was nice and warm making my dick feel like it was gonna bust out my pants. Before I could pull it out, Chas had done it for me. She unbuckled my jeans then unzipped them. I slid my hand into my pocket and pulled out my phone. I went to connect my Bluetooth and went to YouTube. I searched for the song so I could set the mood. Chas was watching me wondering what I was doing and as soon as the song began to play a smile crept up on her face.

I GOT this jones forming in my bones (from a man)
  who indeed took over my soul, (understand)
  I couldn't breathe if he ever said (he would leave),
  get on my knees till they bloody red, (baby please)

SHE PULLED my dick from the top of my briefs and began stroking it. I lifted her body up and slid her down onto my dick. Although her pussy was soak and wet it was still hard for me to get inside. She began panting as she lifted her body up and down to force me inside of her.

"Ohhh Legend." she moaned out softly into my ear. Once I was all the way in, Chas took the initiative and began riding it slowly. I held onto her waist and guided her up and down. Her pussy felt so good she had me ready to bust prematurely. It was warm and tight just how I had left it.

"Damn, I miss this pussy. Promise you'll never leave me Chas." I kissed into her neck. She stopped moving and I looked up to see what was wrong.

"Promise me you'll never let me leave Legend."

"I promise baby." she bent down to place a kiss on my lips. She began riding it again and we fucked like this for a while until I was ready to tear her shit up.

"Bend over." I told her and helped ease her up off me.

I bent her over and made her face the window. I wanted to catch the last bit of sunset while I hit her doggy style. I held her ass cheeks open and slid every inch into her. She began biting into my finger to keep herself from screaming. I went in and out of her with slow, long strokes. Every time my dick came out I watched as her juices filled it up. She was cumming back to back and that shit was turning me on to the point of cumming.

FEELING the copter make its U-turn, I knew we didn't have much time so I begin speeding up my pace. I wanted so bad to slam into her pussy but I had to remember the baby. Suddenly, Chas began throwing her ass back and each time she went up she did this thing where it felt like she was pulling me in. Her walls were locked tight around my dick and I felt my nut building up. Her moans had grew louder which told me she was cumming. The wetter her pussy got, the harder my dick grew. Not being able to hold back, I shot an entire load up into her and made sure to empty every drop. I pulled out of her and slapped her on the ass.

"When we get home, I'mma tear that shit up so be ready." I told her meaning every word. She fixed her clothing and sat back down beside me. She took my hand into hers and laid her head on my shoulder. I looked out into the air and I felt good about my decision. I had my baby back and I felt at ease.

WALKING INTO THE HOUSE, I was hoping Makalah was sleep so me and Chas could spend some more time together. I couldn't wait for Kalah to see her but I needed her first. I had a nice candlelight setup for her and I was gonna run her a hot bath. Without turning on any lights we headed down the hall towards my room. When we walked in, Chas' eyes lit up just seeing all the candles. I had the room filled with Daisies and just like on the helicopter she looked at me shocked, as if to say, how did I know. *You gone learn baby.* I thought.

I went into the restroom and began running her water. I poured in some therapy bubble bath that Lumida had given me. When I mentioned I was going to get Chas, she was happy as hell. Since the day Chas left, Lumida and Kalah both had been asking about her. Lumida chewed my ass out for fucking Stacy, and Kalah called me every mean person in the book. Get this, when I told Lumida she was pregnant she ran into her room and came back with something. Looking down at whatever it was, I couldn't help but smile. It was a baby sweater that she had been sewing and she told me she knew I was gonna have a child. One thing about Lumida, she was very spiritual. Anytime danger was coming my way she warned me and this was why she kept the white candles burning.

WALKING OUT THE RESTROOM, Chas was standing over by my dresser. She looked over at me holding the sketch of my mother's mask killer in her hand.

"Legend, where do you get this?" she asked shaken. I walked over to her and took the sketching from her hand. I had told Chas about my moms but I never mentioned how she died.

"This the mask the killer wore when he raped and killed my mother." I looked over the sketch then to Chas. Tears began to pour from her eyes like something had tainted her.

"WHAT'S WRONG MA?"

"Legend. Oh my god." she said and clutched her mouth. I knew she was hella sensitive and this was another reason I didn't tell her. She took a seat on the bed as tears rained down her angelic face. She looked at me and I could tell something about this sketch had pained her.

"I have something I wanna tell you." she looked scared.

I took a seat beside her and she looked down into my hand at the sketch. "When I was 12 years old, a man came into my house and raped me. He did this to me for years until I became numb. After he would rape me he would take pictures of me and leave. Legend, this was the same mask he wore." she burst out into another set of tears. The more she told her story the more my insides cringed. I had to tell myself to breathe because I was about to lose it. Not only did the entire subject of rape do something to me but to know Chas went through this killed a nigga more.

I let her catch her breath as I rubbed her back. "One night, my father caught him in my house and killed him. This is why I call my father my hero. If it wasn't for my father I would probably be dead." I continued to rub her back to console her. It all began to make sense. The day we were watching TV and the news spoke about a rape, Chas cried. Not only that but the first time we had sex she was too damn tense. That entire night she cried on my chest and I could tell it was something much more than her giving me her virginity. Or at least I thought her virginity. But how could she have not been a virgin, her pussy was too damn tight.

"Chas, I thought you were a virgin." I mentioned because curiosity got the best of me.

"I am, well was. He did...he did it...he did it to me in the anal." she cried out and dropped her head embarrassed. I jumped to my feet just thinking about my mother's death. During the autopsy they had mentioned severe damage to her anal. I stormed out the room and down the hallway. I needed some fucking air. It was bothering me that I couldn't do anything about it because who could I possibly go after?

I SAT OUTSIDE for so long I didn't realize how much time had flew by until I received a text that made me pull my phone from my pocket and look down at the time. It was a text from an unknown number that read.

. . .

(919) 684-3214: I'm sorry Legend if I scared you off. I can't take back what happened in my past. I hope you don't look at me different. Sad face emoji

I GOT up from my seat and headed into the house in search for Chastity. I needed her to understand I didn't run off because she scared me. I left for air because this shit was too much for a nigga to process. I walked into my room and she wasn't there. I went into the guest bedroom and she was under the cover. I pulled the cover back and her eyes shot open.

"Get up ma. Come to *our* bed." I told her and walked out. Chas was now my bitch and I was done with the games. This was officially her crib and we were gonna raise our children here. Therefore my room was hers and I forbid her to sleep in a damn guest room.

WHEN SHE WALKED into my room, she climbed into my bed. I stripped out my clothes and hopped in bed with her. I pulled her into my arms and begin pouring my heart out to her. I started from when I was a child up until my mother's death. I then broke shit down to her about my father's business and what was done in the slaughter. I also told her about Arian and why I didn't believe in love. However, I promised to take a chance with her.

When she asked about her pops, I really didn't know what to say. I was gonna kill Allen no matter what and little did she know I had him locked away in my black hole. He had been there three days now but I wasn't gonna tell her that. A part of me just wanted to let Kill handle it but I needed to taste this nigga blood myself. No matter how painful it would be to Chas, this shit had to be done. I couldn't let this nigga live, especially after the shit with Brandon. Knowing this wasn't just Allen's normal gambling habit routine and more of a set-up it made shit worse for him.

24

CHASTITY

The next morning, I opened my eyes to the smell of fresh bacon. Kemp, Legend's chef, didn't come but twice a week and today wasn't one of those days. I lifted from the bed and did my normal morning routine. I was drained from last night but I felt like the world had been lifted off my shoulders. I had been wanting to tell Legend about my past so he would understand my actions and why I moved the way I did. It was crazy finding out his mother had went through the same thing so I was sure he understood me. The crazier part is, the fact that the same mask man that had raped me all those years raped and murdered his mom. Just hearing him tell me the story made me cry more. I thought of my father and if it wasn't for him I would be dead just as Legend's mother.

WALKING INTO THE LIVING ROOM, I could hear the sound of a woman's voice. It didn't sound like Lumida and it damn sure wasn't Kalah. I walked further into the room and instantly turned up my nose. It was the same chick Legend had told I was his cousin. Jealousy shot through my body because Legend had no room for more bullshit.

Especially after the night I walked in and he was fucking the life out of a chick.

"I just don't understand why you're treating me like this." she whined.

"Man it don't matter. Just get the fuck out my crib before I blow yo fucking wig back." Legend barked and whatever had him upset with her had to be bad.

On cue, they both looked in my direction and her face instantly frowned.

"Oh, so your cousin still here." she said more of a statement than asking.

"Don't worry bout her. And since you wanna be sarcastic about it, Chastity my bitch and not my fucking cousin."

Her eyes grew wide and I could tell she wasn't used to him talking to her like he was.

When her eyes fell onto my stomach she lost it.

"So it's just fuck me huh? All of a sudden. And she's about to have your fucking baby. I swear Legend you foul as fuck." Her eyes began to fill with tears.

"Nah, not all of a sudden. Since I found out you was backstabbing me and fucking Brandon all along." the look on her face confirmed whatever Legend accused her of. She began biting her bottom lip nervously and guilt took over because she started crying hysterically.

"I'm sorry Legend." she sobbed. A part of me felt bad for her but fuck that; it was time for her go. I crossed one of my arms over each other and shot Legend a look. When he looked at me he must have read the look because he told her leave.

"Leg..."

"He said leave." I told her growing impatient.

"Go to the room and get ready ma. I told you I got a surprise for you. Let me handle her." he walked over and kissed me on the cheek. I accepted his kiss then rolled my eyes at the chick and headed for the room. I stopped by the guest room and grabbed an outfit from the bag that I had left then headed to Legend's bedroom to begin my shower.

ONCE I WAS DONE DRESSING I headed back into the living room to find Legend. He was sitting at the table with a money counter in front of him. I stepped in just as he was putting the last stack into the machine. There was neatly stacked piles, with hundreds on top. It was so much money I was sure he did more than just slaughter cows and pigs. Whatever it was I was hoping he stopped by the time my baby came. I didn't want anything to happen to him because he was pretty much all I had. I loved Legend to death and I would literally die if something ever happened to him.

"YOU READY LIL BABY." he looked up from the table. I loved when he called me that so I instantly started blushing.
    "Yeah."

HE STOOD to his feet and began placing the money into a duffle bag. Once done he threw the bag over his shoulder and carried it to the back. I took it upon myself to head outside so I could feel the sun. It was a pretty day and I was glad to finally be going out into the world with Legend freely.

WHEN LEGEND WALKED out of the house, he grabbed my hand and led me to the car. When he opened my door I smiled and thanked him. He hopped in and did his normal routine. Adjust his music and connect his Bluetooth to his phone.
    "I wanna take you shopping. Get you and Makalah some stuff but we will go after this."
    "I'm with you babe." I buckled my seatbelt and we pulled out his spiral driveway.
    "Hold up." he reached into the glove box and threw me a blindfold. Looking at him puzzled he began laughing. "Just put it on ma."

he smiled with that sexy grin I loved and he sold me. Putting on the blindfold I felt the car take off.

ABOUT A GOOD FORTY-MINUTE drive I could tell we were exiting the highway because his speed had slowed down. I remained silent, sat back and enjoyed the ride. The entire time he held my hand and it felt great just being in his presence. Finally coming to a complete stop he told me to remove the blindfold. I took in my surroundings but I was confused as to why we were here.

"Legend, what we doing here?"

"Don't trip ma. Get out."

I stepped out of the car and looked over the new remodeled home. It was my old childhood house that I grew up in. Just staring at the house brought back so many memories and y'all know my emotional ass wanted to cry. A lady in a suit stepped out of the house and met us in the front lawn.

"Hey Mr. Gambino."

"How you doing Elizabeth."

"I'm great. And how are you ma'am?" she extended her hand for me to shake.

"I'm fine." I replied shaking her hand nervously. I was still confused as to why we were here.

"Let's head inside." the lady said and walked us inside. The moment we stepped in I looked around the house. Everything was more up to date and they had even added a marble island to separate the kitchen from the dining area. "Here's the deed and the keys." the lady handed me the paperwork instead of Legend along with a set of keys. Reading over the deed, *Chastity Roberts* stood out in big bold letters. I looked up at Legend and he was smiling from ear to ear.

"Oh Legend, you didn't." I hugged him joyfully. He had brought my old home and this was the best gift I could ever receive. "Thank you so much." I continued to hug him.

"Thank Liz, she made all this happen ma." I turned to the lady and begin thanking her.

"You're welcome. Oh, and before I forget, the workers found that box in the attic. It's been here a while because it's dusty as hell." she chuckled and headed for the door.

"You guys enjoy your home and thank you again Legend." he nodded his head and she left leaving us alone.

"I don't know how to ever repay you. This was big of you."

"You're welcome ma. And you gone be paying me with that." he smiled and rubbed between my legs.

"I love you Legend Gambino."

"Love you too Chastity Gambino." he smirked. When he let me go, both our eyes fell onto the box the lady said that was found. Legend walked over to it and tried to open it but there was a small keypad. He began playing around with it but he couldn't figure out the code.

"Try my mom's birthday. 1-1-69."

He tried those numbers and it didn't work.

"Try my grandpa birthday. 8-10-39." Again it didn't work.

"Try my birthday."

He began entering the numbers for my birthday and turned to ask me what year was I born. Laughing, I gave him my entire birthday and he entered it into the lock. The sound of it clicking was confirmation my birthday worked.

OPENING THE BOX, Legend looked at me and my heart dropped. Inside was a mask but not any mask. It was the same mask that the man wore that raped me and his mother. Sitting the mask on the table there was a bunch of pictures. One by one I picked them up and it was photos that were taken during my rape. My insides instantly began to cringe. The next set of pictures is what got me. There was pictures of my mother and they were taken with a polaroid camera. The same camera used on me. Every position and every frame that was captured was the same replica of all my photos. My heart was beating fast and tears began to pour from my eyes. I looked at Legend not believing my eyes.

"My father." I said just above a whisper. Not being able to hold it in any longer I fell to my knees and began crying hysterically. How could he? Oh my god how could he Legend!" I cried with my face buried into the palm of my hands. "I was a child. I was only a child." I sobbed as Legend fell to his knees and began massaging my back. I couldn't believe this shit. All these years, all this time I thought he was my hero and he was the one that was taking my innocence.

"It's okay baby, I shot that bastard." my father wrapped me in his arms and held me for a split second. Pulling me from his embrace, he looked over my body and his eyes held so much sorrow. "Chastity, you go get cleaned up. I'm gonna go get rid of his body okay."

"We have to call the police." I began to hysterically cry. I was so overwhelmed that my body continued to shake profoundly.

"No baby, we can't call the police. They will take Daddy to jail. You don't want me to go to jail forever right?" I shook my head no sadly.

I BEGAN to think of the night and the more I thought of it the harder I cried. My father had lied to me about killing the man when all along it was him. This was the reason he didn't want to call the police. "God noooo!" I screamed out heartbroken. I looked over at Legend and the look on his face made me remember, my father raped his mother also. All along my father was the Grim Ravasher.

25

LEGEND

Like I said before, God puts people in your life for a reason. He knew what he was doing when he brought Chas into my life, and I was grateful. We were both young and innocent kids that suffered from something so tainting. Although Chas suffered more scars than I, I was still battling with the thoughts of my mother's death. All along, it was her pops who was going around raping and murdering women. Not only that but he was gruesome enough to take pictures. Not only did this nigga murder my mother, rape Chas but he also was the one that killed his own wife. All that bullshit about someone breaking in to rob her was fiction. I couldn't believe this shit.

When Chas spoke on her pops she spoke on the nigga as her hero, but nah, that nigga was more like a fucking walking nightmare. I mean, I know I killed people and did shit that was a sin, but this was an innocent child we were talking bout; his own flesh and blood. Even now, she was so delicate and fragile like a fine piece of China; the shit killed me to know she had to go through that shit.

As I stated, my gut was telling me to just kill him and I guess this was the reason why. They say the Lord works in mysterious ways and now I'm a firm believer. Had I not copped Chas her old crib we wouldn't have known shit. I can't even front, as I held her in my arms, a lone tear slid down my face. I hadn't cried since my mother's death. The shit made my body do something I've never felt; I was beyond 38 hot.

SO HERE I WAS, speeding down I-485 tryna get to my crib. From time to time, I stole glances at Chas who had finally cried herself to sleep. When I pulled up, a part of me didn't want to wake her but I had to. I began to tap her lightly until her eyes shot open. I told her to head into the house. I needed to go holla at Kill. She opened her door and before she got out she looked me in the eyes.

"Legend, I love you." her angelic voice held so much sorrow. It was something about that look that told me she knew what I was up to. And for the first time, she didn't seem to care. She cared more about my well-being and that made me feel more optimistic.

"I love you more ma." I replied then waited for her to enter the house. The moment the door closed I pulled out of the driveway and headed for the Slaughter.

WHEN I PULLED UP, I took a moment to myself and began doing my breathing tactics. My blood was boiling and my hands began to shake from anticipation. Finally gathering myself, I went into the Slaughter and straight for the butchering room. I grabbed the biggest butcher knife we had then headed towards the black hole. The minute I stepped inside I flicked on the light and closed the door behind me. Wasting no time, I walked over to Allen who slept on the cot. I kicked him so hard he jumped up frantically. His eyes fell on the butcher knife I was holding and I could see the fear all over his face.

"Take yo clothes off." I ordered and he began scrambling to get them off. When he was done undressing I made him stand up.

"Man I could pay you back. Please just give me a chance." he began crying like the hoe he was. That tough nigga shit was gone and I was sure my facial expression told him I was over serious.

"This ain't bout no fucking money. This shit deeper than money. You see, Allen, niggas like you don't deserve to live but I decided I'mma let you live. However, I gotta make sure yo bitch ass never use this again." I lifted the knife and with one hard chop I chopped his dick off. He looked at me like he couldn't believe what I had done then his eyes fell onto the ground where his dick laid leaking blood.

"Argggghhh!" he screamed out but his screams were muffled due to the padded walls.

"That was for you raping yo own fucking daughter you sick bastard." his eyes shot open again and the look of guilt took over his expression.

"This one for my mother hoe!" I shouted again as I chopped off his hand.

"Ahhhhhh!" he tried to grab his now missing hand with his other hand. As blood began to squirt from his hand, I raised my knife and chopped the other one off.

"And that one is for your wife." I threw the knife down to the ground as Allen continued to scream. I walked over to the secret door and hit the button. When the door opened I walked towards the entrance door and before I walked out I turned back to Allen.

"I could have easily killed yo bitch ass but nah, you deserve suffering and pain. Oh, and if you think about going to the cops trust me you'll be dead by the time you make it there. And if you ever in yo fucking life as much as call Chastity I'mma kill you. She's dead to you nigga so remember that." And with that, I walked out the black hole and locked the door behind me. I headed for my whip and jumped in feeling ten times better.

After all these years I had finally found the peace I needed knowing I found my mother's murderer. Although Chas would still have to suffer, I was gonna do everything in my power to ease her pain. This was the end of the hurt but a new start for us. I've made up my mind and I was gonna make her my wife. Chastity deserved a happy ending and in due time she was gonna have it.

EPILOGUE

"**B**y the power invested in me I now pronounce you husband and wife! You may kiss your bride" Reverend Jackson smiled and nodded his head to Legend. As tears flooded my face Legend looked me in my eyes lustfully. He then pulled me into his embrace and began kissing me so passionately I got lost in our kiss.

"HE HE HE HE." The sound of snickering made us look over. Makalah was giggling as she sat in the front row next to Lyfe who was in his car seat. Legend and I both looked over and we couldn't help but chuckle. That damn girl was so goofy. Makalah was living with and Legend even changed her last name, Denise has finally come by and when Kalah rued she didn't want to leave, I could tell it took Denise by surprise. However, she agreed to let her stay and basically went on with her life. As for us, we were now married and raising our children. Lyfe was now 8 months and Legend was already trying to get me pregnant again. I finally caught up in school and I was scheduled to take my Bar Exam next month. We never moved into my child home instead we rented it out to a family that worked inside the slaughter. Lately things had been great in our lives and I finally been able to cope with what my father did to me. I must say, I owe it all to my husband because he has done everything in his power to ease my heart of the pain. This was a crazy story and a long ride but for the love I found in not only Legend but Makalah and Lyfe, I'll do it all over again...

THE END

I REALLY HOPE you guys enjoyed this novel. This book had me on an emotional rollercoaster. Things may seem fiction but it's reality. We always fall in love with the ones we're supposed to hate.

PLEASE LEAVE a review on amazon.com and visit my website for new releases, contest and trivia questions.
     www.Authorbarbiescott.com

SUBSCRIBE

Text Shan to 22828 to stay up to date with new releases, sneak peeks, contest, and more....

SUBMISSIONS

To submit your manuscript to Shan Presents, please send the first three chapters and synopsis to submissions@shanpresents.com

CPSIA information can be obtained
at www.ICGtesting.com
Printed in the USA
LVHW111538310519
619751LV00001BA/91/P